# SO BROKEN

(A Faith Bold Mystery —Book Twelve)

BLAKE PIERCE

## Blake Pierce

Blake Pierce is the USA Today bestselling author of the RILEY PAGE mystery series, which includes seventeen books. Blake Pierce is also the author of the MACKENZIE WHITE mystery series, comprising fourteen books; of the AVERY BLACK mystery series, comprising six books; of the KERI LOCKE mystery series, comprising five books; of the MAKING OF RILEY PAIGE mystery series, comprising six books; of the KATE WISE mystery series, comprising seven books; of the CHLOE FINE psychological suspense mystery, comprising six books; of the JESSIE HUNT psychological suspense thriller series, comprising thirty-five books (and counting); of the AU PAIR psychological suspense thriller series, comprising three books; of the ZOE PRIME mystery series, comprising six books; of the ADELE SHARP mystery series, comprising sixteen books, of the EUROPEAN VOYAGE cozy mystery series, comprising six books; of the LAURA FROST FBI suspense thriller, comprising eleven books; of the ELLA DARK FBI suspense thriller, comprising twenty-one books (and counting); of the A YEAR IN EUROPE cozy mystery series, comprising nine books, of the AVA GOLD mystery series, comprising six books; of the RACHEL GIFT mystery series, comprising fifteen books (and counting); of the VALERIE LAW mystery series, comprising nine books; of the PAIGE KING mystery series, comprising eight books; of the MAY MOORE mystery series, comprising eleven books; of the CORA SHIELDS mystery series, comprising eight books; of the NICKY LYONS mystery series, comprising eight books, of the CAMI LARK mystery series, comprising ten books; of the AMBER YOUNG mystery series, comprising seven books (and counting); of the DAISY FORTUNE mystery series, comprising five books; of the FIONA RED mystery series, comprising eleven books (and counting); of the FAITH BOLD mystery series, comprising fourteen books (and counting); of the JULIETTE HART mystery series, comprising five books (and counting); of the MORGAN CROSS mystery series, comprising ten books (and counting); of the FINN WRIGHT mystery series, comprising six books (and counting); of the new SHEILA STONE suspense thriller series, comprising five books (and counting); and of the new RACHEL BLACKWOOD suspense thriller series, comprising five books (and counting).

An avid reader and lifelong fan of the mystery and thriller genres, Blake loves to hear from you, so please feel free to visit www.blakepierceauthor.com to learn more and stay in touch.


ISBN: 978-1-0943-8463-4

**BOOKS BY BLAKE PIERCE**

**RACHEL BLACKWOOD SUSPENSE THRILLER**
NOT THIS WAY (Book #1)
NOT THIS TIME (Book #2)
NOT THIS CLOSE (Book #3)
NOT THIS ROAD (Book #4)
NOT THIS LATE (Book #5)

**SHEILA STONE SUSPENSE THRILLER**
SILENT GIRL (Book #1)
SILENT TRAIL (Book #2)
SILENT NIGHT (Book #3)
SILENT HOUSE (Book #4)
SILENT SCREAM (Book #5)

**FINN WRIGHT MYSTERY SERIES**
WHEN YOU'RE MINE (Book #1)
WHEN YOU'RE SAFE (Book #2)
WHEN YOU'RE CLOSE (Book #3)
WHEN YOU'RE SLEEPING (Book #4)
WHEN YOU'RE SANE (Book #5)
WHEN YOU'RE SILENT (Book #6)

**MORGAN CROSS MYSTERY SERIES**
FOR YOU (Book #1)
FOR RAGE (Book #2)
FOR LUST (Book #3)
FOR WRATH (Book #4)
FOREVER (Book #5)
FOR US (Book #6)
FOR NOW (Book #7)
FOR ONCE (Book #8)
FOR ETERNITY (Book #9)
FORLORN (Book #10)

**JULIETTE HART MYSTERY SERIES**

NOTHING TO FEAR (Book #1)
NOTHING THERE (Book #2)
NOTHING WATCHING (Book #3)
NOTHING HIDING (Book #4)
NOTHING LEFT (Book #5)

**FAITH BOLD MYSTERY SERIES**
SO LONG (Book #1)
SO COLD (Book #2)
SO SCARED (Book #3)
SO NORMAL (Book #4)
SO FAR GONE (Book #5)
SO LOST (Book #6)
SO ALONE (Book #7)
SO FORGOTTEN (Book #8)
SO INSANE (Book #9)
SO SMITTEN (Book #10)
SO SIMPLE (Book #11)
SO BROKEN (Book #12)
SO CRUEL (Book #13)
SO HAUNTED (Book #14)

**FIONA RED MYSTERY SERIES**
LET HER GO (Book #1)
LET HER BE (Book #2)
LET HER HOPE (Book #3)
LET HER WISH (Book #4)
LET HER LIVE (Book #5)
LET HER RUN (Book #6)
LET HER HIDE (Book #7)
LET HER BELIEVE (Book #8)
LET HER FORGET (Book #9)
LET HER TRY (Book #10)
LET HER PLAY (Book #11)

**DAISY FORTUNE MYSTERY SERIES**
NEED YOU (Book #1)
CLAIM YOU (Book #2)
CRAVE YOU (Book #3)
CHOOSE YOU (Book #4)

CHASE YOU (Book #5)

**AMBER YOUNG MYSTERY SERIES**

ABSENT PITY (Book #1)
ABSENT REMORSE (Book #2)
ABSENT FEELING (Book #3)
ABSENT MERCY (Book #4)
ABSENT REASON (Book #5)
ABSENT SANITY (Book #6)
ABSENT LIFE (Book #7)

**CAMI LARK MYSTERY SERIES**

JUST ME (Book #1)
JUST OUTSIDE (Book #2)
JUST RIGHT (Book #3)
JUST FORGET (Book #4)
JUST ONCE (Book #5)
JUST HIDE (Book #6)
JUST NOW (Book #7)
JUST HOPE (Book #8)
JUST LEAVE (Book #9)
JUST TONIGHT (Book #10)

**NICKY LYONS MYSTERY SERIES**

ALL MINE (Book #1)
ALL HIS (Book #2)
ALL HE SEES (Book #3)
ALL ALONE (Book #4)
ALL FOR ONE (Book #5)
ALL HE TAKES (Book #6)
ALL FOR ME (Book #7)
ALL IN (Book #8)

**CORA SHIELDS MYSTERY SERIES**

UNDONE (Book #1)
UNWANTED (Book #2)
UNHINGED (Book #3)
UNSAID (Book #4)
UNGLUED (Book #5)
UNSTABLE (Book #6)

UNKNOWN (Book #7)
UNAWARE (Book #8)

**MAY MOORE SUSPENSE THRILLER**
NEVER RUN (Book #1)
NEVER TELL (Book #2)
NEVER LIVE (Book #3)
NEVER HIDE (Book #4)
NEVER FORGIVE (Book #5)
NEVER AGAIN (Book #6)
NEVER LOOK BACK (Book #7)
NEVER FORGET (Book #8)
NEVER LET GO (Book #9)
NEVER PRETEND (Book #10)
NEVER HESITATE (Book #11)

**PAIGE KING MYSTERY SERIES**
THE GIRL HE PINED (Book #1)
THE GIRL HE CHOSE (Book #2)
THE GIRL HE TOOK (Book #3)
THE GIRL HE WISHED (Book #4)
THE GIRL HE CROWNED (Book #5)
THE GIRL HE WATCHED (Book #6)
THE GIRL HE WANTED (Book #7)
THE GIRL HE CLAIMED (Book #8)

**VALERIE LAW MYSTERY SERIES**
NO MERCY (Book #1)
NO PITY (Book #2)
NO FEAR (Book #3)
NO SLEEP (Book #4)
NO QUARTER (Book #5)
NO CHANCE (Book #6)
NO REFUGE (Book #7)
NO GRACE (Book #8)
NO ESCAPE (Book #9)

**RACHEL GIFT MYSTERY SERIES**
HER LAST WISH (Book #1)
HER LAST CHANCE (Book #2)

HER LAST HOPE (Book #3)
HER LAST FEAR (Book #4)
HER LAST CHOICE (Book #5)
HER LAST BREATH (Book #6)
HER LAST MISTAKE (Book #7)
HER LAST DESIRE (Book #8)
HER LAST REGRET (Book #9)
HER LAST HOUR (Book #10)
HER LAST SHOT (Book #11)
HER LAST PRAYER (Book #12)
HER LAST LIE (Book #13)
HER LAST WHISPER (Book #14)
HER LAST SECRET (Book #15)

**AVA GOLD MYSTERY SERIES**
CITY OF PREY (Book #1)
CITY OF FEAR (Book #2)
CITY OF BONES (Book #3)
CITY OF GHOSTS (Book #4)
CITY OF DEATH (Book #5)
CITY OF VICE (Book #6)

**A YEAR IN EUROPE**
A MURDER IN PARIS (Book #1)
DEATH IN FLORENCE (Book #2)
VENGEANCE IN VIENNA (Book #3)
A FATALITY IN SPAIN (Book #4)

**ELLA DARK FBI SUSPENSE THRILLER**
GIRL, ALONE (Book #1)
GIRL, TAKEN (Book #2)
GIRL, HUNTED (Book #3)
GIRL, SILENCED (Book #4)
GIRL, VANISHED (Book 5)
GIRL ERASED (Book #6)
GIRL, FORSAKEN (Book #7)
GIRL, TRAPPED (Book #8)
GIRL, EXPENDABLE (Book #9)
GIRL, ESCAPED (Book #10)
GIRL, HIS (Book #11)

GIRL, LURED (Book #12)
GIRL, MISSING (Book #13)
GIRL, UNKNOWN (Book #14)
GIRL, DECEIVED (Book #15)
GIRL, FORLORN (Book #16)
GIRL, REMADE (Book #17)
GIRL, BETRAYED (Book #18)
GIRL, BOUND (Book #19)
GIRL, REFORMED (Book #20)
GIRL, REBORN (Book #21)

**LAURA FROST FBI SUSPENSE THRILLER**
ALREADY GONE (Book #1)
ALREADY SEEN (Book #2)
ALREADY TRAPPED (Book #3)
ALREADY MISSING (Book #4)
ALREADY DEAD (Book #5)
ALREADY TAKEN (Book #6)
ALREADY CHOSEN (Book #7)
ALREADY LOST (Book #8)
ALREADY HIS (Book #9)
ALREADY LURED (Book #10)
ALREADY COLD (Book #11)

**EUROPEAN VOYAGE COZY MYSTERY SERIES**
MURDER (AND BAKLAVA) (Book #1)
DEATH (AND APPLE STRUDEL) (Book #2)
CRIME (AND LAGER) (Book #3)
MISFORTUNE (AND GOUDA) (Book #4)
CALAMITY (AND A DANISH) (Book #5)
MAYHEM (AND HERRING) (Book #6)

**ADELE SHARP MYSTERY SERIES**
LEFT TO DIE (Book #1)
LEFT TO RUN (Book #2)
LEFT TO HIDE (Book #3)
LEFT TO KILL (Book #4)
LEFT TO MURDER (Book #5)
LEFT TO ENVY (Book #6)
LEFT TO LAPSE (Book #7)

LEFT TO VANISH (Book #8)
LEFT TO HUNT (Book #9)
LEFT TO FEAR (Book #10)
LEFT TO PREY (Book #11)
LEFT TO LURE (Book #12)
LEFT TO CRAVE (Book #13)
LEFT TO LOATHE (Book #14)
LEFT TO HARM (Book #15)
LEFT TO RUIN (Book #16)

**THE AU PAIR SERIES**
ALMOST GONE (Book#1)
ALMOST LOST (Book #2)
ALMOST DEAD (Book #3)

**ZOE PRIME MYSTERY SERIES**
FACE OF DEATH (Book#1)
FACE OF MURDER (Book #2)
FACE OF FEAR (Book #3)
FACE OF MADNESS (Book #4)
FACE OF FURY (Book #5)
FACE OF DARKNESS (Book #6)

**A JESSIE HUNT PSYCHOLOGICAL SUSPENSE SERIES**
THE PERFECT WIFE (Book #1)
THE PERFECT BLOCK (Book #2)
THE PERFECT HOUSE (Book #3)
THE PERFECT SMILE (Book #4)
THE PERFECT LIE (Book #5)
THE PERFECT LOOK (Book #6)
THE PERFECT AFFAIR (Book #7)
THE PERFECT ALIBI (Book #8)
THE PERFECT NEIGHBOR (Book #9)
THE PERFECT DISGUISE (Book #10)
THE PERFECT SECRET (Book #11)
THE PERFECT FAÇADE (Book #12)
THE PERFECT IMPRESSION (Book #13)
THE PERFECT DECEIT (Book #14)
THE PERFECT MISTRESS (Book #15)
THE PERFECT IMAGE (Book #16)

THE PERFECT VEIL (Book #17)
THE PERFECT INDISCRETION (Book #18)
THE PERFECT RUMOR (Book #19)
THE PERFECT COUPLE (Book #20)
THE PERFECT MURDER (Book #21)
THE PERFECT HUSBAND (Book #22)
THE PERFECT SCANDAL (Book #23)
THE PERFECT MASK (Book #24)
THE PERFECT RUSE (Book #25)
THE PERFECT VENEER (Book #26)
THE PERFECT PEOPLE (Book #27)
THE PERFECT WITNESS (Book #28)
THE PERFECT APPEARANCE (Book #29)
THE PERFECT TRAP (Book #30)
THE PERFECT EXPRESSION (Book #31)
THE PERFECT ACCOMPLICE (Book #32)
THE PERFECT SHOW (Book #33)
THE PERFECT POISE (Book #34)
THE PERFECT CROWD (Book #35)

**CHLOE FINE PSYCHOLOGICAL SUSPENSE SERIES**
NEXT DOOR (Book #1)
A NEIGHBOR'S LIE (Book #2)
CUL DE SAC (Book #3)
SILENT NEIGHBOR (Book #4)
HOMECOMING (Book #5)
TINTED WINDOWS (Book #6)

**KATE WISE MYSTERY SERIES**
IF SHE KNEW (Book #1)
IF SHE SAW (Book #2)
IF SHE RAN (Book #3)
IF SHE HID (Book #4)
IF SHE FLED (Book #5)
IF SHE FEARED (Book #6)
IF SHE HEARD (Book #7)

**THE MAKING OF RILEY PAIGE SERIES**
WATCHING (Book #1)
WAITING (Book #2)

LURING (Book #3)
TAKING (Book #4)
STALKING (Book #5)
KILLING (Book #6)

**RILEY PAIGE MYSTERY SERIES**
ONCE GONE (Book #1)
ONCE TAKEN (Book #2)
ONCE CRAVED (Book #3)
ONCE LURED (Book #4)
ONCE HUNTED (Book #5)
ONCE PINED (Book #6)
ONCE FORSAKEN (Book #7)
ONCE COLD (Book #8)
ONCE STALKED (Book #9)
ONCE LOST (Book #10)
ONCE BURIED (Book #11)
ONCE BOUND (Book #12)
ONCE TRAPPED (Book #13)
ONCE DORMANT (Book #14)
ONCE SHUNNED (Book #15)
ONCE MISSED (Book #16)
ONCE CHOSEN (Book #17)

**MACKENZIE WHITE MYSTERY SERIES**
BEFORE HE KILLS (Book #1)
BEFORE HE SEES (Book #2)
BEFORE HE COVETS (Book #3)
BEFORE HE TAKES (Book #4)
BEFORE HE NEEDS (Book #5)
BEFORE HE FEELS (Book #6)
BEFORE HE SINS (Book #7)
BEFORE HE HUNTS (Book #8)
BEFORE HE PREYS (Book #9)
BEFORE HE LONGS (Book #10)
BEFORE HE LAPSES (Book #11)
BEFORE HE ENVIES (Book #12)
BEFORE HE STALKS (Book #13)
BEFORE HE HARMS (Book #14)

**AVERY BLACK MYSTERY SERIES**
CAUSE TO KILL (Book #1)
CAUSE TO RUN (Book #2)
CAUSE TO HIDE (Book #3)
CAUSE TO FEAR (Book #4)
CAUSE TO SAVE (Book #5)
CAUSE TO DREAD (Book #6)

**KERI LOCKE MYSTERY SERIES**
A TRACE OF DEATH (Book #1)
A TRACE OF MURDER (Book #2)
A TRACE OF VICE (Book #3)
A TRACE OF CRIME (Book #4)
A TRACE OF HOPE (Book #5)

# PROLOGUE

Barrett stared down the barrel and allowed his breathing to slow. His eyes focused on the target, but his training allowed him to see everything surrounding the target just as clearly. There was an obstacle in his way, but if he aimed just right, he could hit the target without interference.

He shifted just slightly, relaxing his muscles to the left rather than tensing them. He took a breath and let it out slowly, then took another. When he took the third breath, he tensed slightly, drawing back and preparing to shoot. As he exhaled, he shot.

The cue ball sped forward, impacting the eleven ball at the precise spot he hoped and spinning it rapidly in a clockwise direction. The eleven ball curved around the eight ball and landed in the pocket just before the cue ball impacted the eight ball.

"Eight ball, side pocket!" Barrett called out just before the eight ball followed its companion into the side pocket.

Barrett and the others watched with bated breath as the cue ball slid toward the corner pocket. It slowed gradually and came to a stop just before momentum carried it into the pocket.

The others cheered, all except for Staff Sergeant Willy, who lifted his hands in frustration and shook his head as Barrett took a bow. He smiled, though, and was the first to shake Barrett's hand. "Good game, Owl. I guess you still got it."

Barrett grinned at his old friend and clapped the man on the cheek. "'Til the day I die, Willy. Come on, I'll buy you a drink for being a good sport."

"Yeah, with *my* money," Willy said, handing Barrett the twenty he had wagered on the game.

"What would you have spent it on?" Barrett challenged.

"Good point," Willy admitted.

Barrett bought the drinks and the two men watched as Sonny Boy—real name Carlo Santino—and Private Smoke—real name Winston—played the next game. When Smoke shocked everyone by coming from behind and beating Santino, the group cheered again, and Smoke bought the whole platoon a round.

Barrett enjoyed these reunions. Sometimes it was hard to remember that there were good things about the Marine Corps, that it wasn't all blood and dust and death. Hanging out with the boys and enjoying good company and good drinks reminded him that for all they had lost overseas, they had gained a family that truly was closer than blood.

His smile faded as he thought of Corporal Carter. The kid had been one of the most promising young men Barrett had ever worked with, but like so many promising young men, he hadn't been able to cope with what he had seen, what he had *done.* So, less than a year after getting his discharge papers, Corporal Carter had drunk a half a fifth of tequila and driven his brand-new Toyota Tundra into an elm tree and finally bid goodbye to the demons that refused to release his soul.

Barrett lifted his drink and said softly, "To Carter."

There would be occasions when the whole platoon would toast Carter and everyone else who had fallen, at home or abroad, but today was a day of fun, a day to celebrate life, not to mourn death. He wouldn't somber the mood by bringing up the fact that so many weren't around anymore to celebrate life.

As he finished his fifth drink, he felt fatigue settle over him and decided it was time to head home. He bought a final round for the boys and girls of Platoon C, Bravo Company, and headed outside.

The night was cool, the humidity just high enough to lend a crispness to the air but not high enough to chill him through his fatigues as he began the trek to his house. The cold sobered him just enough to keep him from stumbling, but enough alcohol remained to brighten the colors and make the world appear more vivid, more *real.*

No one talked about it, not among the boys anyway, but that was the worst part of coming home—the nagging sense that somehow the world around you wasn't the real world but a dream that their minds had created to cope with the fact that they were surrounded by death and violence. Barrett struggled with this dissociation as much as anyone did, but at the moment, with his body warm and relaxed, a night of laughter and camaraderie behind him and the soft, bright lights of home all around him, he was fully immersed in the present.

He hummed a tune as he walked, an old marching song that he had learned as a recruit, and smiled. Life was good.

He heard the snap of a branch behind him, and his hackles rose instantly, an instinct honed by his years surrounded by people who wanted him and his brothers dead.

He turned and saw a figure approach. The shadows obscured his face, but Barrett could tell that he was a he and that he had his hands in his pockets.

Barrett squared to the stranger and said, "Howdy there."

"It's me, Owl," a familiar, soft-pitched voice said.

Barrett's eyes widened. "Doc? Well, I'll be damned! I ain't seen you in…"

His voice trailed off when he saw Doc pull something shiny from his pocket. If it had been someone else, someone Barrett didn't recognize, he would have acted sooner, in time, probably, to save himself.

But this was Doc. Doc wouldn't hurt him. Doc was his brother. There was no way—

Then Dock struck. Barrett's hands moved without conscious thought, parrying the blow.

Too late. The blade slide easily in between Barrett's ribs. He felt the knife pierce his heart and cried out as pain shot through him.

As quickly as Doc had stabbed him, he withdrew the knife, shoving Barrett to the ground and moving on at the same steady walking pace with which he had approached.

"Doc," Barrett mumbled thickly. *Why?*

He didn't manage to get that last word out audibly. The light from the streetlamps twisted and rippled as his vision faded, and the last thing Barrett saw before the light faded entirely was the image of his one-time friend slipping into the shadows.

# CHAPTER ONE

Franklin West approached the door and knelt quietly as though tying his shoe. He had to act quickly. This was the most dangerous part of the job. If anyone saw him jimmying the lock on the door, they would know that he had no business being there, and if the police showed up before he was finished, he was done for.

He slid the bobby pin and jeweler's screwdriver into the lock and smiled. Faith had actually taught him how to do this, though she probably didn't realize it at the time. In one of their sessions back when West was masquerading as a psychologist, Faith had mentioned that she had taught herself to pick locks in case she needed to get past a locked door on a case. West had asked her how she had done it, feigning simple curiosity, but he made sure to commit every step to memory.

This served him well now. The door popped open and West quickly entered and closed the door.

Now, he needed to act very swiftly. Turk was a trained K9 unit, and his age and numerous injuries over the years, first as a Marine Corps K9 and then as an FBI K9, had done nothing to dull his senses. If West wasn't careful, Turk would kill him.

Franklin West, known to the wider world as the Copycat Killer, had held Turk before. He could have killed Turk then, but at the time, he thought leaving the dog alive was necessary to keep Faith from imploding and becoming uninteresting. Faith, however, had proven far more resilient than West expected. Worse, she had been far too comfortable remaining outside of the investigation. Before, she had blatantly ignored orders to stay away.

And that wouldn't do. West needed his attention to be on her. Nearly killing the boyfriend hadn't been enough, but killing her dog would.

And he needed to succeed this time. Not even a chance that Turi might survive.

He rushed into the kitchen weapon at the ready. Turk's sleeping silhouette was just visible in his bed. West launched forward, driving the tip of his knife toward the base of Turk's skull.

Turk opened his eyes and met West's own. For a split second, West watched gleefully as the dog's eyes widened in shock.

Then Turk moved so swiftly that West couldn't follow it. He leapt from the bed and West's knife buried itself harmlessly in the bed.

"Shit!" West cried, spinning instantly to his knee and slashing forward with the knife, keeping the snarling Turk at bay. "Fuck! Goddammit!"

If West could admit to any weakness, it was that he handled disappointment poorly. He was an exceptional planner and equally exceptional at executing those plans, but when things didn't go his way, he was easily angered.

The vet's survival had affected him this way, but he had quickly reasoned that this would work out better for him in the end.

The dog, though, he needed to go. Faith would not break as long as Turk was here. He needed him to die, *needed* it, and now the goddamned dog had ruined everything.

Turk snapped at him and West thrust with the blade, aiming for the Shepherd's neck. Turk once more displayed shocking agility, twisting in the air and avoiding the blow without slowing his own strike.

West swore again, diving just past Turk's snapping jaws and rolling to his knees, knife held in front of him. How was Turk so much faster? The last time the two had fought, West had stopped him almost effortlessly. Was Faith's absence allowing Turk to move more quickly since he didn't need to focus on her safety as well as his own?

"Goddammit, you little runt!" West snarled, thrusting again and again with the knife. Turk continued to dodge the thrusts, but West kept cutting the animal off, forcing him to back against the wall. West began to calm slightly. He was still winning. This wouldn't be the clean kill and clean escape he had hoped for, but he would still win. He just had to be patient.

And, of course, that was when the door opened, and Faith Bold walked into the apartment.

***

Faith considered herself to be a fairly lapsed former Marine. She rarely thought of her time in the Corps and was infrequent in her contact with her former brothers- and sisters-in-arms. It wasn't that her time in the Corps was unusually painful for her—if anything, her tenure in the FBI had been far more traumatic—but she was so wrapped up in her job, especially over the past few years, that she rarely had time for anything else.

But the instincts she started developing nearly fifteen years ago remained as sharp as ever. As soon as she saw West, knife outstretched and pointed at Turk, she moved without thinking. Her right knee collided with West's jaw before the surprised criminal had a chance to turn his weapon. He cried out and stumbled backwards, and Faith ducked and spun, sweeping his foot from underneath him.

He fell heavily, but moved with lightning quickness, regaining his feet and thrusting first at Turk, then at Faith to keep them at bay.

"You goddamned bitch!" he growled. "You fucking whore!"

His normally calm, smug face was twisted in a mask of rage, and Faith felt a rush of triumph. After years of torture at the hands of the Copycat Killer, she was finally going to bring him to justice.

"Give it up, West," she said. "We have you this time."

West reddened the color of a beet, then calmed. He smiled, baring his teeth and said, "I was supposed to have you. Your dog, rather. I must say, well done. The lad is trained far better than I expected him to be."

Faith would have had Turk tear West's throat out if it wasn't for the knife West had leveled against him. Instead, she flanked him, moving carefully so as not to allow him a chance to escape. "Franklin West," she said, "you're under arrest for—"

"Oh please, Faith, aren't we past that? Come on, hiding behind professionalism? Surely you can do better than that."

"I'm not playing games with you this time, West," she said, "put the weapon down and surrender yourself."

Later, Faith would allow herself to feel the shock and fear and violation that would come with knowing that West had been in her house about to kill Turk, but she kept those emotions at bay for now. She needed to call for backup. She had West now, had him dead to rights. If she could hold him here while she waited for the police to arrive, he would have no chance of escaping this time.

"West, be smart about this," she said, "You have no chance of escaping. Put the weapon down."

West looked between the two of them, eyes narrowed, lips pulled back in a snarl. Faith felt a rush of triumph at the desperation in his eyes. All the time she had known West as the killer, she had never seen him this out of sorts. If she could keep him backpedaling, she could bring him in. This could end today.

West chuckled. "We seem to be at an impasse, Faith."

"No impasse, West. You have a knife. I have a dog and a gun. You lose. Put the knife down and surrender yourself."

West grinned. "Very well."

With a lightning-fast strike, he swung the blade in an arc toward Turk's neck. The angle of his blow forced Turk to leap to his left to dodge, blocking Faith's shot at West.

That split second was all West needed. He sprinted past the two agents, shoving Faith to the ground as he rushed for the door. Turk barked and sprinted after him, but West swung around, once more slicing with the knife. Turk came to a halt, and West continued on his way. Faith tried to aim, but West disappeared into the shadows, and she lost her bead.

"Dammit," she swore, following Turk from the apartment and calling, "West! Stop, or I swear to God I'll shoot you!"

She felt the hair on the back of her neck stand up and spun around to see West dive into a car on the opposite side of the street. She swore again and lifted her handgun, firing twice. The first round shattered the rear windshield and the second buried itself somewhere in the cabin, but West gunned the motor and the car leapt around, heading straight toward Faith.

She and Turk dove to the side, and the car narrowly missed them. She rolled to her feet and aimed again, but West caromed around the street corner and sped off, leaving them behind. The car's license plate had been removed, and it was the most common model of automobile in the United States. There would be no way to track him.

Turk started after him, but there was no way he was running down a car, and she didn't want to risk West running him over if he tried, so she called him back.

Turk stopped a few yards ahead of her, and both agents listened in frustration as the sound of West's fleeing automobile faded.

# CHAPTER TWO

"Here, drink this."

She sipped the liquid, and warmth infused her. She hadn't realized how cold the night was until she sipped the coffee Michael brewed her. Like all of the coffee Michael made, this brew was far stronger than it needed to be, but it was also far more flavorful than the cheap swill she kept in her pantry. "Guatemala?" she asked.

"Bali, actually. But you were… well, not close at all, but I'll forgive you, all things considered."

He smiled lamely, but Faith couldn't manage a return smile. As the adrenaline from her recent encounter with West faded, her frustration and fear gradually grew strength.

He was in her house. He was in her *house*, dammit! He had nearly killed Turk!

"They'll get him," Michael said, reading her thoughts. "He can't be that far away. They'll find him."

"He's never been far away," Faith said. "He's been here in Philadelphia the whole damned time. He won't run, he'll hide. He's good at that. He's probably already in disguise, safe somewhere in whatever home he's taken while he waits for a chance to—"

"Faith," Michael said sternly, cutting through her emotion. "Take a breath."

*"You* take a breath!" she snapped. "You didn't walk in on a serial killer holding a knife to your dog's throat!"

Michael's interruption served its purpose despite Faith's retort. Her mind left the runaway train of irritation and began to think clearly. "I'm sorry," she said, "I'm just pissed off."

"I don't blame you," Michael replied. "I'm pissed off too."

"That makes three of us," another voice said. "Goddammit, how did he get into your house?"

Special Agent Desrouleaux approached the three of them, his face red with anger. Desrouleaux was the current lead on the Copycat Killer case and as far as the FBI was concerned, the one ultimately responsible for bringing Franklin West to justice. He was clearly unhappy with the fact that his quarry was not only not in hiding in the far-flung reaches of the world as he and his team believed but in fact less than three miles from the field office where he and a team of agents worked round the clock with representatives from multiple other law enforcement agencies to hunt him down.

"Are you asking me or just blowing off steam?" Faith asked.

"I'm just pissed," Desrouleaux said. "This guy's been making an idiot out of us for years now. How the hell does he keep doing this?"

"I wish I knew," Faith said. "If it makes you feel better, he fooled me too. I never thought he would try to attack Turk in my own house."

Desrouleaux sighed. "Well, he's not getting in again. We're going to station two agents here and two agents on the street behind you. West tries to get in again, and he's going to end up looking like Swiss cheese."

Faith's phone rang, and she frowned when she saw the Boss's number. "Bold."

"Bold, get to the office. I have a case. Bring Prince."

She took a breath, "Sir, I'm dealing with a situation right now."

"No, I am. Desrouleaux will handle things there, and we're posting agents to watch your house. The best thing for you professionally and personally is to be as far away from here as possible. So, I'm sending you to solve a case in Washington State."

Faith's lips thinned. "Sir, my life was personally threatened today."

"That only supports my point," the Boss replied. "Look, Faith, you know your history with this guy. You know that you can't be around anything that smells like the Copycat Killer."

"Sir," Faith said, struggling to remain patient. "In the past six months, he's nearly killed me twice, nearly killed my dog twice—invading my home the second time—killed one of my old friends and one of my new friends and nearly killed my boyfriend. I can't keep ignoring this."

"You can and you will. You've already said you think he's trying to draw you out. If you let him, then you're playing right into his hands."

"And how many more people need to die to protect me?" she challenged. "I say give him what he wants. Let him see if he can really hurt me the way he thinks he can."

"This isn't up for discussion, Bold. I'm sorry about what happened tonight, but putting you on the case is *not* the answer. We'll have people watching your house, and we'll have people watching your boyfriend at the hospital. Now get to the office. I promise you, you won't be happy if I have to come to you."

Faith sighed. There was no point in arguing with the Boss. “Yes, sir.”

She hung up, and Michael said, "He's right, you know. You'll be a lot safer if you—"

“How about you stop there?” Faith asked.

“Sure,” Michael said, lifting his hands placatingly. “I just want you to be safe.”

Faith decided it was pointless to argue with Michael too and let the comment slide.

***

Special Agent-in-Charge Grant Monroe—known affectionately as the Boss to his Philadelphia Field Office employees—wore his trademark scowl when Faith and Michael entered his office. Turk barked formally, and the Boss nodded with equal formality, an adorably absurd interaction that would have brought a smile to Faith’s face any other day.

Today, it did nothing to change her irritable mood. She understood where the Boss was coming from. West had managed to kill one of their best agents already and had made a career out of making the rest of them look like fools. Even the New York Field Office eventually gave up, turning the case back over to the Philadelphia office.

So she could understand his desire to protect her, but it frustrated her that she was being forced away from an investigation into a man who had grown obsessed with harming her and her loved ones.

When she and Michael were seated, the Boss dropped two different folders on the desk in front of them. Faith lifted an eyebrow as she took one, and Michael took the other. "Are we splitting up?" she asked the Boss.

“No,” he said, “You’re solving another cold case that has decided to become hot again.”

Faith opened her file and saw a familiar set of pictures and findings. “The Miller case?” she asked. “That’s back on the table?”

The Miller case was a murder in the small town of Miller, Washington, where a small-time arms dealer was found stabbed to death outside of a gas station with the word VENGEANCE written above his head in his own blood. Local authorities feared a surge in organized crime violence and asked the FBI for help, but after three months of extensive casework, the FBI had found nothing.

“That was over a year ago,” Michael said, “and what does it have to do with a war veteran getting killed outside of a bar?”

“Look at the second picture,” the Boss told him.

Michael did and raised his eyebrows. “Ah.”

Faith leaned over to see and wasn’t particularly shocked to see the word VENGEANCE written in the ground above the victim’s head.

“Victim is Barrett Jones,” the Boss said. “He was on his way home after having some drinks with his old platoon and ended up stabbed.”

“What branch did he serve with?” Faith asked.

“Marine Corps.”

Faith's eyes widened, and Turk looked at her. Both of them had served in the Corps too prior to joining the FBI.

“Made it to the rank of Gunnery Sergeant,” the Boss continued. “Left after hitting his twenty years. Combat experience in Iraq and Afghanistan. VA’s being tight-lipped about his psych profile, as usual, but his platoon buddies swear he would never start a fight. Said he came home from the war determined never to fight anyone again. Looks like someone brought the fight to him.”

“Why isn’t CID handling this?” Faith asked, “Or NCIS?”

“They’re saying that it’s our wheelhouse since Jones was discharged. Unless the crime turns out to have been perpetrated by an active-duty employee of the Department of the Navy.”

“Sounds like they want us to do the work so they can take the credit,” Michael said sourly.

“I’ll make sure to put your name in the headline if it’s so important to you, Prince,” the Boss quipped. “In the meantime, you two are to treat this like any other case. If NCIS or CID comes to you and wants a piece of the pie, they have to talk to me, and I’ll remind them that they’re the ones who wanted to give you control.”

The Boss was very influential within the FBI, but if the Department of the Navy wanted the case, he was going to have a hell of a time keeping them from having it. Military agencies didn’t play by the same rules as civilian agencies.

Faith didn't tell him that, though. There was no point, and in any case, if NCIS wasn't already falling all over themselves trying to take this case, then they didn't want it.

“All right,” she said, “I’m assuming we head out now?”

“Yep. Flight leaves in an hour.”

When the three agents left the building, Michael said, "How the hell does he always manage to find a flight that leaves exactly an hour after he talks to us?"

"He probably calls ahead for the tickets after we've already left the office," Faith replied.

Michael's eyes widened. "Huh. That actually makes sense."

"Most things do if you look at them long enough," Faith replied.

"I'm going to come up with an insult to throw back at you later," Michael said, "but right now, I just want to know how you feel."

She chuckled. "Well, I appreciate the question, Michael, but how I feel isn't going to change reality, so it really doesn't matter."

"It matters to me."

She tensed a little. "Michael, I… like I said, I appreciate it, but… please don't pity me right now, okay? I can't handle it."

"Sounds good," Michael said, "How's David?"

Faith glared at him, and he said, "Hey, I like him too."

"You've met him once."

"And I liked him. How's he doing?"

Faith sighed. "He's improving. He actually woke up the other night. Only briefly, and he wasn't fully lucid, but he recognized me, and he… we talked." She didn't want to tell Michael that David had told her he loved her too. She wasn't sure if she was worried how Michael would react to that, but either way, it was a private moment between her and David, and she didn't feel like sharing it right now.

"That's good," Michael said. "I'm glad to hear that. I'm sure he'll pull through."

Faith didn't reply.

Michael allowed her to ride in silence as he drove the three of them to the airport. Faith felt bad about taking her frustration out on Michael, but it was all she could do to manage her own emotions without having to be worried about his.

As they reached the airport and boarded their flight, Faith realized she was actually excited to take this case. She had to admit, albeit grudgingly, that flying away from her problems for a while was a welcome distraction. She chuckled as she thought how less than twenty-four hours ago, she was seriously considering leaving the Bureau.

"Not me," she said aloud. "I'm in it for life."

"What was that?" Michael asked.

“Nothing,” she said, leaning back in her chair and closing her eyes. “I’m going to get some sleep.”

She kept her eyes closed for a while, but in the end, her energy kept her from finding sleep. She gave up and smiled down at Turk, who stared ahead with the same focused intensity. She reached down and ruffled his fur. “Let’s go catch a bad guy.”

# CHAPTER THREE

Faith stood in between Michael and Turk and stared at the body of Barrett Jones.

"Any thoughts?" Michael asked.

"Well," she said, "I'm glad his head hasn't been smashed in."

"Yeah," Michael agreed, "You can say that again."

In their last case, the killer's MO involved bludgeoning young women to death with a baseball bat or tire iron. The results were gruesome, to say the least.

Gunnery Sergeant Barrett Jones was far more presentable than those young women had been, but he was no less dead. The cause of death appeared to be a single, deep thrust to the heart, but most of the blood, including the blood used to write the word VENGEANCE above his head, came from the long grooves cut into his arms from wrist to shoulder and the slit cut across his throat.

"Post-mortem?" Michael asked, pointing to the slit throat.

"I think so," she replied. "The coroner will have to tell us for sure."

Turk approached closely, sniffing the body and looking for clues that he could identify as they investigated. Faith squatted down and took a closer look at the body, putting on latex gloves and lifting Barrett's head, arms and legs, checking for anything that might help them understand what had happened.

"What do you think?" Michael asked.

She sighed and stood. "Well, he wasn't killed here. He was moved."

"From where?"

"I'm not sure," she said. "There's not a lot of blood, but depending on where he was killed, the blood might have just soaked into the ground. He could have been dragged here or brought by vehicle. It's hard to tell."

"I'll order a sweep of this area," Michael said. "We might get lucky and find something. Maybe Turk can look around too."

"That's a good idea," Faith said.

As though on cue, Turk started barking excitedly. Faith and Michael jogged over to him, and Faith asked, "What is it, boy? What do you see?"

Turk stepped back, and Faith stooped to see a small ribbon buried in the muck. She picked it up, and the ribbon turned out to be attached to a bronze pendant. She brushed off as much of the muck as she could and looked more closely at it.

"What is it?" Michael asked.

"It's a meritorious service medal," Faith said.

"Jones's?"

"Maybe," she said. "Or maybe the killers."

She put it in a bag and gave it to Michael. "Have forensics look at this too. We might be able to get some prints off of it."

While Michael took the medal to forensics, she and Turk continued to examine the crime scene and the surrounding area. Faith was sure that Barrett had been moved, but she needed to know how. Knowing how he was moved would help her determine how far away he had been killed, and that could go a long way to helping her find Barrett's killer.

She thought back to the first case, the one in Miller, Washington. The victim then was Geoff Murray, an arms dealer known to have sold weapons to various different terrorist groups over the past twenty years. At one point, rumors existed that Murray had sold weapons to insurgents fighting against American soldiers in Afghanistan. Faith didn't condone his killing, but she understood it.

But Barrett Jones? He was a family man with no criminal record who had served with distinction in the U.S. Marine Corps for twenty years. If he was a highly placed officer who could conceivably have been involved in shady arms dealings or some sort of equivalent national security threat, she could understand why he might have been targeted, but he was an NCO, and not a particularly senior one.

And he had been retired for years.

It was possible that someone had just copied the other killer's MO. She knew very well how often that happened.

But she still didn't know why.

First things first, though, she needed to know where. "Can you smell anything, Turk?"

Turk put his nose to the ground and led Faith away from the crime scene a short distance. Then he barked and jogged up a low embankment. He ran for about a hundred yards before stopping at the edge of the road. Faith could see the bar a quarter mile distant, and when Turk showed her the dried bloodstain on the ground below, she looked back at it in amazement. Someone had killed Jones less than fifteen hundred feet from help then dragged hm another five hundred feet and staged him like some sort of macabre art piece.

She reached down and patted Turk's head. "Good boy."

She tried to visualize the crime. Jones leaves the bar, walking south down the road. He's drunk, so he's probably swaying a little and his awareness is dulled, so he doesn't hear the footsteps walking behind him for a while.

But when he does hear it, his guard would come up. He was a Marine combat veteran. Those instincts never disappeared. He could be at his child's birthday party, and if he hears someone coming up behind him, he's going to be prepared to fight.

Michael joined her a moment later and said, "I guess we found the actual scene of the murder."

"Did Jones have any defensive wounds on his body?" Michael asked.

"CSI says no, but they also say that his nails were cleaned before he died, so they can't tell for sure if he defended himself and the killer disposed of the evidence."

Faith nodded. So either Barrett had tried to defend himself and been overpowered—something that occasionally happened even to Marines—or he hadn't recognized the attacker as a threat. Was that because he underestimated the attacker or because he recognized them?

The coroner wagon arrived a moment later. The coroner, a short, balding man in his fifties, grimaced when he saw the body. "Lovely. Another psycho."

"Get a lot of those out here?" Faith asked.

"Not a lot, but when we do, they're good ones."

"That's encouraging."

"What can you tell us about this psycho?" Michael asked.

"Not much beyond the fact that he *is* psycho. As soon as I have anything, I'll let you know." He shook his head. "Damn. I was a kid when the soldiers came home from Vietnam. I didn't know any of the politics, but I remember being really sad that everyone was being so mean. Little did I know."

Faith and Michael left CSI to wrap up the scene and headed to the bar. That was the last place Jones had been seen alive. Hopefully someone there would have information they could use.

A neon sign announced the bar's name as the Happy House and featured an image of a girl in a miniskirt lifting her legs to show what was underneath. There weren't any poles inside and no sign of topless servers, so it wasn't a skin bar like she would have assumed from the look of it.

Faith was hoping to get contact information for Jones' friends, but when she walked inside, she saw three different people in Marine Corps uniforms sitting at the end of the bar. When they looked up and saw the FBI agents, their eyes widened, and they left their drinks and approached Faith and Michael.

"You're the ones looking into Barry's murder?"

The speaker was a tall, barrel-chested individual with the stripes of a First Sergeant. He was the highest-ranking person present, and though they were all officially civilians now, they still deferred to him.

"That's us," Faith replied. "Special Agent Faith Bold." She extended her hand, and the First Sergeant took it. "This is my partner, Special Agent Michael Prince, and my K9 unit, Turk."

The big man nodded. "Any idea what happened to Owl?"

"We're following up on some leads," Faith said, not wanting to share too much information yet. "May I ask your names?"

The big man nodded again. "I'm First Sergeant Orrin Trask." He gestured to a short, stout man to his left. "That's Staff Sergeant William Porter, and this—" he hooked his thumb to a petite, athletic woman about ten years older than Faith who stood on his left, "Is Corporal Candace Rogers. We all owe Owl our lives."

"Owl?" Michael asked.

"That was Gunny's nickname," Candace answered. "We called him that because he had sharp vision and Hawk and Eagle were already taken. Also, the enemy called him Silent Death because he killed from thousands of yards away."

"He was a sniper," Faith said.

"Yeah. Best in the business. When our unit was pinned down, he shot all five of the machine gunners dead before they even knew what was happening."

"After that, we told Colonel Muskrat we had to have him," William said.

"Muskrat?" Faith recognized the name. "Janice Musgrove?"

Orrin's eyes widened. "Yeah. You know her?"

Faith grinned and rolled up her sleeve. When the others recognized the eagle, globe and anchor tattoo, their demeanor changed instantly. The three of them brightened, and Rogers laughed. "I should have known you were a Marine. I could see it in your eyes. What unit were you?"

“Delta Company, 5th Battalion, 22nd Infantry Brigade,” Faith replied. “Staff Sergeant, but I spent most of my time in the suck as a corporal.”

“The workhorses of the Corps,” William said with a grin. “I was a Corporal in the suck too. Bravo Company, 4th Battalion, also 22nd. How’d you know Muskrat?”

“She came by to visit us at the MCGACC just before we deployed,” Faith said. “I remember thinking she looked like a beaver. That was before Decker told me her nickname.”

“Holy shit, you know Decker?” Candace said, “I went to boot with Decker! How is he? I haven’t seen him in years.”

Faith’s smile faded, and the other Marines knew the answer before she said it. “Gone. Different killer.”

“Goddammit,” Orrin said. “Why the hell did we travel halfway around the world to risk our lives so we could come home and get killed here?”

“People don’t fuckin’ understand,” William said. “They hate war, and because they hate war, they hate us. Like we’re the ones sitting in a fucking air-conditioned office deciding we need to go fight over a bunch of sand dunes in Asia.”

“Most people aren’t like that,” Faith said, “Most people appreciate our service.”

“Yeah? Tell that to Decker and Owl.”

The five of them fell silent for a moment. Candace broke the silence. "You need a drink, Staff Sergeant. Then we'll toast Owl and Decker. Your boyfriend can drink too if he wants."

“Oh, I’m not… thanks,” Michael replied.

Faith suppressed a smile as the three Marines led them to the bar. When all had drinks in hand, Orrin lifted his glass. “To Staff Sergeant Decker.”

The five of them drank and William followed the toast by saying, “To Gunny Owl, the best damned sniper the Corps ever knew.”

“Hear hear,” Candace seconded.

They drank again, and with the toasts completed, Faith got to business. “What time did Owl leave the bar?”

“Ten-thirty,” William replied. “He wasn’t much of a late-night person anymore after his kids were born. Had to be up early to get them ready for school and stuff.” He ran his hands through his hair. “Oh God, his kids. Fuck, someone has to tell them.”

“PD already did,” Candace said, “Leah called me this morning. The kids are at her mother's place in Vancouver. She's here taking care of the arrangements."

“Who’s helping her?” Orrin asked.

“Sonny Boy,” Candace replied. “His cousin works at the memorial. He’s taking care of all the paperwork so they don’t give her any trouble over the plot.”

“They better not give her any trouble,” Orrin said darkly. “Or I swear to God, I’ll light asses from here to Washington.”

“Nah, Sonny’s cousin is a good guy,” William reassured him. “He’s Army, but don’t hold that against him. He’ll take care of Owl.”

“What about after?” Orrin asked.

“Smoke’s gonna help with chores,” Willy said. “I’ll be there every weekend to get the kids out of the house. We’ll go to the zoo and stuff, take their mind off of things.”

Michael shifted impatiently in his stool, but Faith shook her head at him. They would get the information they needed, but they couldn’t interrupt grieving Marines. This was how they processed the loss of one of their own. She and Michael were going to have to wait no matter what.

“I just don’t get it,” Orrin said. “Who’s out here killing Marines?”

"So far, his murder is the only murder of a Marine by this killer that we know of," Faith said.

“Yeah, but it won’t be the last,” Candace said grimly. “You know that.”

“Well, it’ll be the last in my platoon,” Orrin promised. “From now on, we’re never alone. We always go out with a buddy, and no one comes within striking distance unless you know them.”

“That might be a problem,” Faith said. “We think Owl might have been known to the killer.”

“Well, it couldn’t have been someone from the unit,” Orrin replied. “They were all here.”

“So you can’t think of anyone who might have wanted to hurt Owl?”

“No one specifically,” Orrin replied, “but there’s a particular class of people who doesn’t like warfighters but don’t have a problem killing one.”

“We don’t believe this was politically motivated,” Faith assured him.

“Whatever it was,” Orrin replied, “that asshole better hope he never gets within a hundred yards of any one of us.”

"I know this is tough, First Sergeant," Faith said gently but firmly, "but we're home now. We're not on reservation, and we're not in the suck. You need to let us handle it."

“Because you’re a Marine,” Orrin replied, “I’ll accept that. But find this asshole,” he said, “and make him pay for thinking he can hurt my Gunny.”

“I will,” she said, “I promise you that.”

# CHAPTER FOUR

The next morning, Faith and Michael visited the coroner's office bright and early. Talking with Owl's platoon mates hadn't provided any more information. No one saw what happened to Owl when he left the bar because he had done this several times before and had always been fine.

Knowing that this was a pattern of his was helpful, however. It was likely that this killing was planned and not opportunistic. Now she just had to figure out why someone would kill an international arms dealer and a Marine Corps sharpshooter in the same manner within a dozen miles of each other but over a year apart.

Hopefully the coroner would have some helpful information for them.

The coroner turned out to be a silver-haired woman of around sixty named Doctor Joyce Townsend, who greeted the agents with a sad smile.

"It's always a pity when it happens to one of our boys," she said. "It's bad enough you have to fight in the suck, then you come home and get killed by a psychopath? It's bull!shit."

The curse was incongruous with Doctor Townsend's age and dignified manner of carrying herself, but Faith understood perfectly. "Did you serve?"

"4th Mechanized," Townsend replied. "I was a gunner in a Bradley in Somalia and a Stallion in Kosovo. Got out just before the 9/11 attacks. Tried to go back after the towers fell, but they 4-F'ed me because I have a plate in my knee." She tapped her knee, the hollow clang illustrating her point.

"22nd Infantry Brigade," Faith replied. "I'm hoping you can help me figure out what happened to our boy."

Townsend sighed. "Well, the wound that killed him was the one to his heart. The killer slid the knife directly in between the ribs and pulled it out without even nicking the bone. The rest of the cuts happened about thirty minutes to an hour after death."

"So after he was moved."

"Yes. About that, he was carried, not dragged."

Faith lifted an eyebrow. "How much does he weigh? Two-twenty?"

"Two-sixteen," Townsend replied. "Our killer would have to be strong, but if he knew body mechanics, he wouldn't have to be impossibly strong. The knife wounds were more about precision than strength."

"I noticed that," Faith said. "Was our killer a medical professional?"

"I think so," Townsend replied. "I don't know that for sure, obviously, but these cuts are almost surgical. Even the way he cut the throat was designed to avoid the tough tendons that surround the carotid and jugular."

"Why go to all this trouble?" Michael asked. "When it would have taken so much less effort to just kill him?"

"That's a question for the detectives," Townsend said, nodding to the two of them. "I would say that the killer was trying to send a message, but I don't have a damned clue what that message was supposed to be."

"Vengeance," Faith said, "but for what?"

They left Townsend after extracting a promise to call them the moment she had anything and headed to a coffee shop in town. Pembroke, Washington was the next town over from Miller, another piece of evidence that suggested that the killer of that arms dealer was the same as the killer who murdered Jones.

While they sipped their coffees, Turk enjoying a cup of whipped cream—which the barista called a "pupuccino—" they discussed next steps.

"These two victims are connected," Faith said. "There may be a substantial gap in their deaths, but I'd wager anything it's the same killer and not a copycat."

"Why do you say that?" Michael asked.

"The MOs match."

"We could be looking at another copycat."

"For one murder of a victim who wasn't well-liked? It's extremely unlikely."

"Then why the gap?"

" I think that the killing last year might have been spontaneous."

Michael raised an eyebrow. "The killer spontaneously wrote the word vengeance over Geoff Murray's head?"

"Maybe spontaneous is the wrong word," Faith admitted, "but I think our killer wanted it to be a one-time thing. I don't think he was looking to make a career out of killing people."

"So what made him start again?"

"I don't know," Faith said, "but I know he's not done."

"You're sure of that?"

She nodded. "The first time he killed, he probably spent months afraid he'd get caught. Or she. I suppose it could be a woman, too. Possibly the spouse of someone who was killed overseas."

"I could understand the arms dealer if that was the case," Michael said, "but not Jones. Correct me if I'm wrong, but no military wife I've ever met would want to murder a fellow Marine."

"None that I've ever met," Faith said. "Not an NCO, anyway."

"They'd kill the officers?"

"Some of the upper-level brass could move to the next world without driving me to tears," Faith admitted, "but no, it's not likely that our killer was a military spouse."

"So what are we looking at?" Michael said.

"I think we need to stop trying to find a conclusion and start looking for evidence," Faith said. "The fact is we don't have enough information right now to identify a suspect."

"So where do we start looking?"

"Let's start with the Murray case from last year. That was the first killing and the most likely to have a clear motive."

They looked through the file, and Faith noticed something in Murray's bio. "Hold on. Murray was a Marine, too."

Michael's eyes widened. "He was?"

"Yes. He lasted about a year before he was discharged for lying on his application."

"Probably about his citizenship," Michael surmised.

"And his name. And his social security number. Probably all sorts of identity problems."

"So was there overlap? Did someone know both victims?"

They continued to dig, and after another hour, Faith found something. While searching for Geoff Murray's name online, she came across several articles written by a journalist names Ariel Pena, an investigative reporter for the *Seattle Post* who had taken it upon himself to prove that Geoff Murray was trafficking arms through Washington State. While looking up Pena, Faith found that he had been jailed twice, once for trespassing on private property she claimed belonged to Murray and refusing to leave until the police removed her, and one for assault.

Apparently, Mr. Pena had taken issue with someone calling her a left-brained kook and had decided to express his displeasure by hitting the offender over the head with a fast-food tray. Apparently, the *Seattle Post* didn't care about hiring violent employees because they had no problem letting Pena keep his job.

Faith skimmed a few of the articles, and the evidence grew more and more damning. Pena ranted about the purveyors of death and how they were destroying their safe, beautiful communities. He argued that the military should be disbanded and that anyone who owned a gun was a murderer whether they used the weapon or not because they were supporting the creation of weapons designed to kill. In several of the articles, he suggested that those people should use their weapons on themselves or else allow others to do so.

"I'm starting to like Mr. Pena," Michael said. "He seems like the kind of person who would consider himself justified murdering a man for no good reason."

"Let's reserve that call for when we talk to him," Faith said, "but I'm starting to like him too."

The agents called the Post and learned that Pena had, in fact, been fired, although it had taken the paper six months after the assault charge to do so. The reason they gave was "frequent attendance and reliability issues," but Faith had a feeling there was more to it than that.

They got his last known address and headed over. Faith felt a rush of excitement now that they were finally heading to a suspect's house. In her experience, the first suspect was rarely the final one, but they had a direction now, and even if Pena wasn't their killer, he had done a lot of research into their first victim. His information could prove valuable as they tried to make sense of what had happened to first Murray and then Gunny Jones.

***

Pena seemed to have slipped further into whatever insanity had prompted his eccentric behavior and inflammatory writing. His house was in a fairly advanced state of disrepair when they arrived, at least judging by the exterior appearance. The chain link fence surrounding the property was nearly overrun with vines, and through the open gate, Faith could see the lawn was nearly two feet high and choked with weeds three times that size. The house was nearly as overrun with vines as the fence, and the roof was missing several shingles. If it weren't for the relatively clean pickup truck in the driveway, Faith would have thought the place abandoned.

Michael sighed as he parked across the street. “Wonderful. I’ll just bet this guy’s a nice, calm, well-mannered dude who won’t give us any trouble whatsoever.”

Faith smirked. “Why? Not fancying the fisticuffs anymore, old man?”

“Nope,” Michael said emphatically. “I’m a cordial conversation guy these days. Besides, my head still hurts from last time.”

In their last case, Faith and Michael had gotten into physical confrontations with three of their subjects. It didn’t help that all three suspects were very strong and athletic. Faith herself still carried a few bruises from those encounters.

“Well, Pena’s listed as five foot ten and one-sixty, so I don’t anticipate the same kind of trouble from him.”

“Bruce Lee was five-foot-eight and one-forty. He’d have kicked both our asses and Turk’s too without breaking a sweat.”

“Well,” Faith said drily. “If Pena turns out to be the next Bruce Lee, I’ll pay for your medical care.”

"Damn right, you will."

The three of them approached the front door. Pena’s yard smelled as swampy as it looked, and Faith wondered how much worse the inside had to be.

Well, they were about to find out.

Faith knocked on the door while Turk and Michael prepared to respond in case Pena reacted dangerously. Faith motioned for them to be calm and waited.

The door creaked open, and Pena poked his head out. His eyes were filmy and bloodshot, but even if they were bright and clear, Faith would have smelled the alcohol emanating from him like cologne. He looked between the two agents, blinking at the bright light of the day. “Who are you?” he finally asked.

"I’m Special Agent Faith Bold of the FBI. This is my partner, Special Agent Michael Prince, and my K9 unit, Turk.”

“Okay,” Pena said.

“We’re here investigating the murders of Geoff Murray and Barrett Jones,” Faith said. “We need to ask you a few questions. May we come in?”

She watched Pena’s eyes carefully. He betrayed no sign of recognition at the names, but considering his inebriated state, he might not be entirely lucid. She wondered if it would be better to take him to a drunk tank and let him sober up before they talked.

Pena blinked again and finally said. “Yeah. Sure.”

He turned and shuffled inside, leaving the door open for them to follow. Turk trotted in first, his head down as he sniffed for clues. Faith and Michael shared a look, then followed him inside.

The inside of the house wasn’t nearly as dirty as Faith expected. The sink was empty of dishes, and it exhibited at least a token effort at tidiness.

It was dark, though. The curtains were all drawn, and the only light came from a floor lamp with a single incandescent bulb. Though the house was clean, the musty odor that first assaulted Faith’s nostrils in the yard was stronger inside the house. Faith wondered when Pena had last opened his windows.

“You want coffee?” Pena asked. “Or beer?”

“I’m all right, thank you,” Michael said.

Michael never refused coffee, so he must have been as put off by the smell as Faith was. She pushed that feeling to the side and reminded herself that she’d dealt with worse. In a recent case, the three of them had chased a killer through a massive cave system. She’d take a dimly lit room with a musty smell over the darkness of that cave any day.

They sat at the table and waited while Pena poured himself a very tall glass of tequila. “Would you mind waiting to drink until after we finish talking?” Faith asked. “These questions are very important.”

Pena shrugged and left the glass and the bottle sitting on his counter, then took a seat opposite the detectives.

“Thank you for taking the time to talk to us,” Faith began. “Can you verify your whereabouts yesterday evening?”

“Yesterday? I was at the bar.”

“Which bar is that?”

“The Happy House. Used to be a strip club, but the new owner didn’t want to pay the taxes for a place like that, so he just turned it into a bar.”

Faith felt a leap of excitement. So Mr. Pena was at the same bar where their victim was murdered.

“What time were you there last night?”

Pena shrugged. "I don't know. Late. I go there after work, and then I usually stay until the place closes."

“Where do you work?”

"Junkyard. I used to be a reporter, but nobody wants to read my stories anymore."

"We've read a few," Michael told him.

Pena perked up slightly. "Oh yeah? What did you think?"

"We'll get to that," Michael said. "Why don't you tell us more about your visit to the Happy House last night?"

Pena shrugged again. "I mean… I drank."

"Fascinating," Michael said drily.

"You said you normally stay until the bar closes," Faith said. "What time did you leave last night?"

"I don't know. Early."

"How early?" Faith asked patiently.

He shrugged once more and shifted in his seat. Faith could see he was getting nervous. "I don't know. There were a bunch of soldiers in the corner celebrating something. I don't like soldiers, so when I figured out they were gonna be there all night, I left."

"They were Marines," Faith said, "not soldiers."

He blinked. "Well, they looked like soldiers. What's the difference?"

"Different branches," she said. "Did you see any of the Marines leave before you did?"

"I don't know. I don't like soldiers."

"You've said that twice now," Faith pointed out, choosing not to point out a second time that they were Marines and not soldiers, "but you haven't told me much else."

"Well, I don't know. Like, why would I pay attention to them? I told you, I don't like soldiers."

"And now you've said that three times," Faith replied. "Here's the thing, Mr. Pena: those articles that Special Agent Prince and I read make it very clear that you don't like soldiers. They also make it clear that you feel soldiers should be killed with their own weapons. Now, as I said, those men and women were Marines, not soldiers, but seeing as how you have trouble understanding the difference, a part of me wonders if you might have decided to take the opportunity to enact some of the justice you call for in your articles."

Pena blinked. "What?"

"One of those Marines was murdered last night," Michael said. "That was Barrett Jones. We think you might have had something to do with it."

Pena's eyes widened, and a few layers of intoxication melted away in the face of his fear. "What? Because I wrote some angry articles?"

"Some *very* angry articles," Faith emphasized, "and very graphic. Not to mention that you had a vendetta against Geoff Murray, the arms dealer who was murdered here in Miller just over a year ago."

"What?" Pena cried, another layer of intoxication falling away. "Murray was a prick! He was selling guns to kids to make a quick buck. I couldn't believe no one arrested the asshole. He wasn't even being subtle about it. He deserved to die."

"So you took matters into your own hands," Michael suggested.

"Yeah!" Pena said. Then he realized what he'd said and added, "Wait. No! I didn't kill him. I just told people to kill him."

"Who?"

"Not like a person. Like the whole public. Like, we should all kill all those assholes."

"Including soldiers?"

"Hey, look, we live in America, right? We're safe here. But what about other places? What if we go to China where our soldiers can just walk into people's homes, kill their families and get away with it? We shouldn't stand for that, right?"

"You might want to do a little research on some of those claims," Faith suggested, "but I see your point. They're evil, right? They deserve to die."

"Exactly!"

"So maybe you killed them. Maybe you saw your chance with Murray and Jones and you took care of the problem yourself."

"Man, I didn't kill anyone, okay?"

"So here's my concern," Faith said, folding her hands on top of the table and staring frankly at Pena. "You wrote a series of articles advocating violence against people involved in warfighting. Then a known arms dealer who recently moves to Miller ends up brutally murdered with the word vengeance written over his head. Fast forward to last night, you're in a bar with several members of the military—people who you argue should be murdered—and one of them ends up murdered in the same manner as Murray with vengeance also written over his head in his own blood. You admit that you left early because—and you were very clear about this—you don't like soldiers. So maybe you're heading home, and you see that one of these men who you hate so much is walking home too. Maybe this is your chance. Maybe you can finally do what you've been telling everyone to do. You already got rid of the arms dealer, and no one caught you. Maybe they won't catch you this time."

“That’s not fucking true!” Pena shouted.

Turk growled low in his throat, and Pena paled.

“Let’s go back a bit, then,” Faith said. “We’ll leave last night for now and go back in time to thirteen months and nine days ago.”

“Man, I don’t remember where the hell I was back then,” Pena said.

The fog in his eyes had completely cleared by now. His eyes were wide as saucers and shifted right and left. He rocked back and forth in his chair and tapped his right heel on the ground, and several times, he looked over at the front door as though wondering if he could make it before the agents could stop him. Faith pushed her chair back from the table, preparing to tackle him if she needed to. Michael noticed and stood, moving behind Faith so he could respond too if needed.

Pena’s eyes snapped to Michael, who smiled and explained, “Bad back. Standing’s easier.”

Pena nodded, and Faith said, “You need to try to remember, Pena, because you don’t have a good explanation for last night.”

Pena sighed and said, “Look, the shit I write, I mean that figuratively. Like, I’m not actually saying that people should go kill soldiers, I’m just saying that it’s wrong that people are revered as heroes for causing wars and killing people. I think they should be hated. I think they should all be hated until we get peace in this world.”

“Well, hate does have a good track record at creating peace,” Michael deadpanned.

“Hey, fuck you!” Pena said, turning aggressive on a dime. “Don’t stand there and talk down to me like I’m the stupid one! If you didn’t have a fucking gun in your vest, you wouldn’t talk to me like that.”

“Why?” Michael asked. “What would you do to me if I did?”

Pena’s eyes narrowed, but he had enough presence of mind not to reply.

“Have you always had a problem controlling your anger, Mr. Pena?” Faith asked.

“You know what?” Pena said, “Fuck you too.”

“All right,” Faith said, standing. “I hoped we could have a conversation here, but since you’re being uncooperative, we’ll have to have this conversation at the station. Please stand and put your hands on top of your head.”

"What?" Pena's anger vanished, replaced by fear. "Wait, no. Look, okay! I'll talk! I was on my way to Murray's house the night he was murdered!"

"What for?"

"To talk to him! To interview him!"

"You were going to give him a platform?" Faith asked. "Forgive me if I don't believe that."

"I wasn't going to give him a platform, I was going to trip him up. I was going to ask him questions and make him admit to being evil. Then I was going to give that evidence to the police. But as I was driving to his house, I got nervous, okay? I thought that maybe he'd just kill me if he didn't like what I had to say. So I turned around and went home. On the way back, I saw him dead, and I freaked out because I thought whoever killed him might still be there."

"Did you report the body to the police?"

"Hell no! I didn't want that coming back to me."

"Can anyone verify that you were home?"

Pena moaned and ran his hands through his hair. "I don't… wait! Yes!" His eyes lit up with a joy and relief that was almost comical. "Yes, I was on the phone with my brother the whole drive home! You can call him or look up the phone records or something. He heard me freak out when I saw the body! He might even have heard my truck engine when I hit the gas. Those diesels are loud. I don't know, but maybe."

Faith and Michael looked at each other. "Turk," Faith said, "Watch him. If he moves, take him down." She turned to Pena. "My partner and I are going to step outside and discuss this briefly. Stay seated where you are. If you make trouble, you will absolutely be placed under arrest. Do you understand?"

Pena shook his head up and down so fast Faith thought it might fly off. "I won't move. I promise."

Outside, Michael asked Faith, "What do you think?"

Faith sighed. "Well, we should follow up with that phone call, but I buy it."

Michael's eyes widened. "Really? He seems very unstable. I could see him flying off the handle and stabbing someone to death for very little provocation."

"I could see that too," she admitted, "but he's also skittish and paranoid. I can't see him killing someone within view of a public road and a bar, then dragging the body into the bushes, carefully, surgically cutting the body and leaving a message written in the victim's own blood. That takes a lot of calm under pressure. Pena doesn't show me any of that calm."

Michael sighed. "Yeah, good point. Well, let's get the phone number and follow up with the brother and the phone company. If their story matches his, we'll move on."

# CHAPTER FIVE

Leah Jones was in predictably poor shape when they arrived at her home. Her face was red and puffy, and her shoulders hitched with sobs. No tears fell, but her eyes were red and swollen, and Faith thought she had probably shed all the tears her body could produce right now.

The soldier with her was confrontational at first, insisting that she be allowed to bury her husband before she was harassed by law enforcement, but when Faith revealed her history as a Marine, he calmed down, and she learned that he was Carlo Santino, Sonny Boy to his brothers.

"You found anyone yet?" he asked.

"Not yet. We had a suspect, but his alibi turned out to be airtight."

Sonny sighed. "All right."

"We'll find him," she said, "I promise."

He managed a half-smile. "All right. Come on in. I'll take you to see Leah. Just be gentle with her, okay?" he asked. "She's taking this hard. He was home, you know? He was supposed to be safe."

"I'll be gentle," Faith promised, "but the faster we work, the more likely we will be to catch Owl's killer before he or she can kill anyone else."

Sonny nodded. "All right. Yeah, just be gentle."

She laid a hand on his shoulder. "Hey," she said softly. "You're doing a good job. They'll be okay, Leah and the kids."

Sonny sighed. "I know. This just sucks. Dammit, we're home. We made it through the suck, and now…" he lifted his hand and let it drop.

"I know," Faith said. "Don't worry. We'll get this guy."

He nodded and offered her a half-smile before turning to Leah. "I'm going to go pick up some food for dinner tonight. I'll be back soon, okay?"

Leah nodded and tried to smile, but she couldn't quite manage it.

When Sonny left, Faith offered a sad smile of her own and said, "I'm sorry for your loss and sorry that I can't offer you anything more helpful than that yet."

"It's all right," Leah said, "There's nothing you could have done to stop it."

“No,” Michael agreed, “but we can bring the killer to justice.”

Leah nodded. She showed no sign of relief at hearing that. Maybe she never would. It might bring some measure of closure to know that the person responsible for her husband’s death was being brought to justice, but it wouldn’t bring her husband back. Her children still wouldn’t have a father. They would still be left with a hole in their lives, and the best they could hope for was that the hole would become a scar and not continue to bleed.

Faith sat on the edge of the couch and folded her hands on her lap. Turk sat next to Leah and looked up at her with his sad brown eyes while Michael stood with his head bowed and his hands clasped in front of him. The four of them waited in silence a moment, mourning Jones’ loss, then Faith began.

“Mrs. Jones, I’m sorry to have to ask this, but can you think of anyone who might want to hurt your husband?”

She shook her head. “Not in this country. There’s probably some people in Iraq and Afghanistan who don’t like him, but not people who would come here to find him. Just enemy soldiers fighting for their land.”

“So you never received death threats or threats of any kind from people back home?”

“No,” she said. “No, everyone was very kind and appreciative for the most part. You run into people every now and then who are anti-military, but all the people I talked to were angry at the brass, the generals, you know, not us.”

“What about from his past?” Michael asked.

Leah’s brow furrowed. “His past? What do you mean?”

“You married after he joined the service, correct? Did he ever tell you anything about his life from before you two met?”

“Um… I mean, just the normal stuff. He never mentioned anything about anyone hating him.”

“Did he ever talk about his job in the military?”

She laughed softly, the ghost of humor that she no longer felt. “No. Most soldiers don’t. They don’t want to talk about what they had to go through. What they had to do.”

“I understand that,” Faith said. “I don’t like to talk about it either.”

“I don’t blame you,” Leah said. “I hated that he had to do that. I was proud of him for doing it, but I hated that he had to. It’s so horrible that people have to go fight and kill and die just to be allowed to live in peace. Then we still can’t live in peace.”

She closed her eyes, and tears trickled down her cheeks.

"Does the name Geoff Murray mean anything to you?" Faith asked.

"Geoff Murray?" she shook her head. "No. Should it?"

"Geoff Murray was an arms dealer who lived in Miller just up the road," Faith explained. "You never heard your husband talk about him?"

She shook her head again. "No. Is he the one who stabbed Barry?"

"No," Faith said. "He was killed last year in a manner very similar to your husband. We're trying to understand why someone might have wanted both of them dead."

"Is there always a reason?" Leah asked. "Sometimes, I just think people are crazy."

"There's always a reason," Faith confirmed, "but sometimes it's a reason that we can't understand. Not on the surface, at least. But we're trying to understand this one."

"Did your husband spend a lot of time out of the house?" Michael asked. "Maybe go places he didn't talk about?"

"I mean… he would go to the bar at least once a week. The Happy House. It's on the forty-two."

"We've been," Faith said.

"But he would only go there to visit his friends. Sonny Boy and Smoke and Candy—they all have nicknames, you know."

"Yes," Faith said. "Nowhere else, though?"

"No. Just the bar and home. I mean, we'd take the kids out and stuff, but he was never without me unless he was with the platoon at the bar. He worked out of the garage, but he had a pension and a lot of benefits due to his service, so he really only did favors for friends. He liked motorcycles. He built custom frames and bodies and stuff like that."

Faith sat back and tried to hide her frustration. It happened frequently that victims were connected in ways that only mattered to the killer, and occasionally, those connections weren't understood until they found the killer, but in those cases, there were always multiple victims. It was difficult to act quickly when there was no logical reason for the victims to both be targeted.

"How did your husband seem lately?" she asked. "Any difference in mood, changes in behavior?"

"No, he seemed normal. I mean, he had his down days, but everyone did when they came back from the war. I never got the sense he was suicidal or anything, and I never got the sense he was afraid."

“You said he was at the bar at least once a week,” Michael said. “Was he usually there more often?”

“I mean, maybe two or three times.”

“Was he ever drunk at home?”

“Not in front of the kids,” Leah said. “He would go to the bar after the kids went to sleep and be sober the next morning. But I mean, he fought overseas.” She looked at Faith. “You understand.”

“I do,” she said, “and I don’t mean to suggest that your husband was in any way immoral or a bad person. It’s perfectly common for people to struggle with depression after serving.”

“But he didn’t seem depressed. I mean, he was always smiling and happy. I know that sometimes people still smile when they’re depressed, but…” she blushed slightly. “Well, we had a good love life. I don’t feel like he could be so… energetic if he was depressed.”

“We’re not suggesting that he committed suicide,” Faith said. “It’s very clear that wasn’t what happened here. What we’re trying to determine is if something happened that caused a change in his behavior that might indicate fear for his life or just general fear.”

“Well… one of their friends had died recently. James Carter, like the President. He died in a drunk driving accident a little over a year ago. Barry cut back on his drinking a lot after that. He stopped driving when he was drunk too. The bar’s only a mile up the road, so he’d walk there and walk back. I told him I could pick him up, but he said he liked the walk because it could help him clear his mind. He never seemed afraid of anything, though. He just… I figured he missed Jimmy, and this was his way of talking to him.”

“And they’re sure it was an accident?” Michael said, “Carter’s death?”

Leah smiled bitterly. “He was nearly four times the legal limit when he hit an elm tree at eighty miles per hour. So yes, they’re pretty sure it was an accident.”

Faith and Michael shared a look. Michael’s compassion was mixed with frustration at his own helplessness.

Faith understood. There was nothing he could do, less, because while he had endured his own share of trauma, the suffering that combat veterans endured was something that only combat veterans understood.

Faith understood. She reached forward and laid a hand on Leah’s shoulder. “I’m sorry for your loss, ma’am. Your husband was a hero. And he will always be a Marine. If you ever need help with anything, please don't hesitate to ask. It's not just Barry's platoon that will answer the call. You have two hundred thousand brothers and sisters who will support you."

Leah gave Faith the first real smile Faith had seen since the three of them arrived. "I know," she said, "I'm so glad that his legacy will be honored."

Faith returned a smile of her own. "Count on it."

The three agents drove in silence back to the hotel. It wasn't until they parked that Michael said, "You know, you never talk about your time in the Corps."

"No," Faith agreed. "I don't."

She left the car, leading Turk into the hotel without another word.

# CHAPTER SIX

Doc sat in the van and pretended to focus on the meatball sub he was eating. In reality, his eyes soaked in every inch of his surroundings.

The world was full of innocent people and equally full of the guilty who loved nothing more than to prey on the innocent to slake their thirst for blood. The problem was that most of the guilty were exceptional at hiding in plain sight. They would pretend to be innocent and fill their time with seemingly mundane activities, leaving no one the wiser that while they were hurting and killing and plotting to hurt and kill more and more?

A mother walked by holding hands with a young girl of five or six. The girl smiled brightly at him, waving her hand and saying something that Doc couldn't hear through the window. He returned the smile and the wave, and the girl beamed and skipped along after her mother.

Her oblivious mother, whose gaze had never once lifted from the phone she held.

God, that pissed him off. Couldn't she see? Wasn't she aware that the world was filled with murderers? How did she know that the three teenagers lounging against a tree with their skateboards weren't talking about how they were going to massacre the students at her daughter's elementary school? How did she know that the electrician fixing the streetlamp next to the marketplace wasn't rigging a bomb to go off at the height of everyone's winter shopping spree?

All around the killer, he saw danger. There were the men in expensive suits who spoke in low voices and frowned darkly at anyone who approached. Mafiosos plotting their next hit? Even the parents could be murderers. For all Doc knew, that woman was engrossed in her cell phone because she was texting a hitman to make sure her husband would be dead by the time she got home.

He wished he could stop them all. If he were in another part of the world, it would be easier. He could carry the appropriate tools for the job and do away with these assholes without having to worry about being stopped by overzealous fake champions of the law.

But he was limited to other tools, tools that were designed to save lives.

He focused on the light pressure of his favorite tool in its wrist scabbard, safely ensconced behind his long-sleeved shirt. No one ever anticipated the need for a sheath for a scalpel. After all, scalpels were to help keep people alive. Why would anyone need to hide that intention?

He had learned the hard way that sometimes, to keep people alive, you needed to kill other people. The scalpel was doing its job. It was saving lives. Just not in the way it was intended.

Unfortunately, that meant it was only useful when he was up close and personal with a target and only on one target at a time. It meant he had to attack in the shadows and not in the light.

He didn't mind that part. He had been brainwashed into learning how to do that.

And now he was using himself, a tool of the warmongers, and the knowledge those warmongers gave him to do his part in ending the wars that claimed far more people than he ever would.

His target was in line to buy a pretzel. He wore a white polo shirt and tan khakis over brown leather work boots. He was fit and trim, though even from this distance, Doc could see the softness in those gym muscles. He had perfectly coiffed blonde hair and a pair of sunglasses that probably cost most of that mother's food budget for a month.

He wore an easy smile as he chatted with another customer waiting for his pretzel and Doc's blood boiled. God, why could no one else see it? He was even baring his teeth, the classic sign of a predator!

Well, it was okay. His job was to serve and protect those who couldn't protect themselves. The warmongers had given him that job, though they, of course, intended a different application.

Still, he operated under the spirit of that oath. He grinned as he recalled the faces of the warmongers who had already tasted his justice. Another one would taste it soon.

The target received his pretzel and moved away. He would walk to the opposite end of the strip mall and pick up his dry cleaning, blithely ignoring the sign that requested he leave his food outside. He would then stop by the liquor store for a bottle of mid-range Scotch, which he would parse out over the next week. He would then buy a bouquet of flowers and a box of chocolates so his wife would remain blind to his actions.

Then he would go home, watch a movie, make boring, predictable love with said wife, shower and go to bed.

Then he would wake up and plea for Washington to start more wars and send more people to die so the poor impoverished defense conglomerates could continue to sell stealth fighters, tanks, guns and ammunition to people like him who would be brainwashed into murdering people for money.

But not for much longer. The killer knew enough now to know how to stop him. He had his plan, and now he knew how to execute it.

He finished his meatball sub, carefully wiped the sauce from his hands and face, and put the van in gear. He pulled out of his pot, careful not to upset the other tools he had in the back of the van, and headed home.

*Enjoy your pretzel, warmonger,* he thought.

# CHAPTER SEVEN

They started the next day by visiting the crime scene where Geoff Murray was killed. The gas station had closed down only a few weeks after the murder since locals understandably gave the place a wide berth. The former owner had been cleared in the initial investigation and had promptly moved to Florida, so Faith and Michael didn't follow up with him other than to confirm with his new employer that he had been at work the day of Jones' murder and couldn't possibly have made it to Washington State in time to commit the most recent killing.

The gas station had, of course, been repainted and cleaned, so they weren't going to find any physical evidence, but Faith wanted to see the scene in person so she could understand what might have happened.

Turk began sniffing for clues. Faith doubted he'd find anything, but she let him look anyway. She and Michael stood in front of the spot where Murray's body had been found and tried to piece together events.

Michael looked at the old case file and said, "Says here that he was murdered across the street and dragged here."

"He was dragged across a busy street?" Faith asked.

"Well, he was killed at two-thirteen in the morning, so the street wasn't busy when he was murdered. But yes, he was dragged across the street and left here."

Faith waited for a break in traffic and crossed the two-lane highway. There was a ditch on the other side of the highway, and when Faith climbed down inside of it, she could see that it was very possible for the killer to have avoided being scene. Bushes lined the upper half of the ditch, concealing her from view and helping to break up any noise the killer might havc madc as hc murdered Murray.

How would he have gotten Murray here, though? Murray wasn't the world's most famous drug dealer, but he wasn't a fool either. He would have insisted on meeting his client and delivering his product on his own terms. Hidden in a ditch on the side of the road at three in the morning wasn't a good term.

She heard Turk bark and climbed up the embankment, jogging across the street back to where Turk and Michael stood. Turk's tail was wagging, and when Faith arrived, Turk dropped what he had found in front of her.

It was a ring. She stooped and picked it up. It was a garishly oversized gold ring with a stone that looked like an amethyst in the middle, although Faith suspected it was just stained quartz.

"Amethyst," Michael said. "I always thought it was crazy that people would spend so much money just for a different color of quartz."

"Is amethyst quartz?" she asked.

"Yep. Just purple quartz. When quartz has iron in it and gets exposed to heat, the iron makes the quartz turn purple."

"Huh," Faith said, "you learn something new every day."

She looked at the crystal and said, "Like, for example, that someone with the initials B.B. was likely present when Geoff Murray was murdered."

"So who's B.B.?" Michael asked.

"Ah," Faith said. "That, my friend, is the million-dollar question."

"So how do we find the answer? We can't talk to Geoff Murray."

"No," Faith said, "but we can talk to someone who knew him. He had a family, right?"

"Surprisingly, yes."

"Why surprisingly?"

Michael looked at Faith. "Are you serious?"

Faith shrugged. "Plenty of evil people had families who loved them. Some of them even knew exactly how evil their spouse, parent, child, or sibling was, but they loved them all the same. Of course, plenty of evil people had families who hated and feared them too."

"Well," Michael said, "let's find out on which side of the coin Geoff Murray's family falls."

***

Few of the surprises Faith encountered in her line of work turned out to be pleasant. So when they looked up Geoff Murray's family and found out that they still lived in Miller, Washington, Faith dared to hope that the tide of the case may have turned. If they could figure out who B.B. was, then they may find their killer before he had a chance to kill anyone else.

The Murrays lived in a rather remote country estate three miles outside of the town proper on a seldom-traveled side road, which is probably why they still lived here. From what Michael could gather from articles, blogs, opinion pieces and public social media records, the family's reputation had suffered greatly in the year since Geoff's death. That was understandable, but still unfortunate for Geoff's children, who were, of course, innocent of their father's crimes.

Geoff's wife, Lindsey, had chosen to homeschool their children upon her husband's death and subsequent exposure, and the family had kept a low profile. Faith wondered why she chose to stay, then realized that any assets her husband might have left her would have been taken. She probably didn't have the financial wherewithal to move.

That might be worth exploring. If she was tied somehow to his business or his money, she could have knowledge of his death that would help them. She might even be the one responsible.

These possibilities flitted through Faith's mind as Michael pulled into the long gravel driveway of the Murray house. The house itself was fairly small for something called an estate, two stories and what Faith guessed to be four bedrooms, but it sat on seven acres of beautiful hillside with a natural pond that occupied one of those acres and a stand of some thirty spruce trees that looked like a miniature alpine forest.

It was an idyllic place to raise a child and an ironic place to reside if one was an international arms dealer responsible for selling weapons to terrorist organizations.

Lindsey Murray answered the door reluctantly and barely made eye contact with the agents as she invited them inside. She was a wan-faced, tired-looking woman of forty-one, not surprising considering she had been left to raise hers and Geoff's four children alone after he was murdered and exposed.

"I don't have any coffee," she said, "but I have green tea if you'd like some."

"That's all right, Mrs. Murray," Michael said. "We won't be here very long."

Turk trotted inside after Michael and looked around, sniffing for clues. Faith brought up the rear, looking around and taking note of the furnishings. They were homey and comfortable, but there was nothing that screamed opulence or excess.

Her suspicions were confirmed a moment later when Lindsey said, "The government took all of the good furniture, but the couch is comfortable if you want to sit."

The agents accepted that invitation and Faith said, "Like my partner said, we only have a few questions to ask." That was true, but part of the reason they had insisted on meeting Mrs. Murray in her house was so Turk could look around for any clues.

Lindsey shrugged. "Stay as long as you need. I'm sure your dog is looking around for incriminating evidence as we speak."

There was bitterness in her voice, but no anger. She had long since accepted that this was her life now.

"Well," Faith said, not confirming or denying the purpose of Turk's continued snooping, "we'll get right into it, then. We believe that the person who killed your husband is active again in the Miller-Pembroke area."

"The soldier who died two days ago?" Lindsey asked.

"The Marine," Faith replied. "Yes."

Lindsey nodded. "I thought he'd come after me, to be honest."

Faith raised an eyebrow. "He?"

"Well, yes," Lindsey said. "Are you telling me a woman did this?"

"We're not sure," Faith replied, "but we're leaning toward a male."

"Me too. Geoff wasn't the world's greatest badass, but he knew how to fight."

There was no admiration or disgust in Lindsey's voice when she said that. She was simply stating a fact.

"Can you tell me what happened the day your husband was killed?" Faith asked.

Lindsey sighed and sipped her tea. A ghost of what might have been grief when it was fresh but was now only wistfulness crossed her face. "He woke up at four-thirty, like he always did, exercised, made coffee and breakfast, ate it with me and our children, showered and kissed us goodbye, like he always did. Then he went to work and didn't come home."

"Where did he work?"

Lindsey chuckled softly. "You don't have to use kid gloves with me," she told the agents. "I know what he was. I always did."

Faith and Michael shared a look. "We're not here to judge you, Mrs. Murray," Faith replied. "We're just here to find the man who killed him and Barrett Jones."

She kept a close eye on Lindsey's face when she mentioned Barrett's name, but Lindsey showed no sign of recognition.

Lindsey smiled. "Of course you're going to judge me. People always do. How do you marry a man like him? How do you allow a man like that to father your children? What about everyone who died because of him?"

Faith kept silent. Lindsey clearly needed to say this, and if it helped her relax, it would help the agents glean any useful information she had.

"The answer, Special Agent, is that I loved him. Have you ever been in love?"

"Yes," Faith replied.

"Then you know what it is to feel so strongly for someone that you'll look past any faults they have to justify staying with them."

*No,* Faith thought. *Not even close.* Aloud, she said, "Like I said, Mrs. Murray, we're not here to judge you. We just need to know who killed Geoff."

"Why? So you can drag his name through the mud again? He loved his children, Special Agent. He was good to me. He donated to charity. He saved far more lives than he killed, and who are we to say that the people he sold to have any less right to fight for their freedom than we do?"

Now it was time to refocus. "Mrs. Murray," Faith said. "I apologize for being blunt, but I'm not interested in hearing you justify your husband's crimes or your choice to remain married to him. That isn't why I'm here. Unless you killed your husband, you have nothing to worry about from me."

Lindsey chuckled. "If *I* killed him. That's funny. Even if I didn't love him, I would never have chosen to put my children through what they've gone through."

"Where are they now, if you don't mind me asking?"

"They're with my mother. You don't need to know where."

"No," Michael agreed, "we don't. Can you tell us who might have wanted your husband dead?"

Lindsey fixed him with a frank look. "My husband sold weapons to labeled terrorist groups. There were governments that had contracts on him. I carry a gun in my purse to this day because I'm afraid of being contacted by some pissed off intelligence agent upset that he didn't get to be the one to put a pulled into Geoff's head."

"Anyone with the initials B.B.?" Faith asked.

"B.B.?" Lindsey frowned. "What's that?"

Faith showed Lindsey a photo of the ring she had found at the crime scene. Lindsey stared at it a moment, then chuckled and said, "This was my husband's ring. The B.B. stands for Big Balls. He got it as a gag gift after an Indonesian warlord held a gun to his head and Geoff told him to put that thing away before he hurt himself."

Her eyes welled with tears. "God. Grief hits you at the strangest times."

Despite her disgust for what Geoff Murray had done, Faith found herself sympathizing a little for Lindsey. Was this what Faith had to look forward to if David didn't make it? Would it be worse or better because she and David didn't have any children?

"Who gave him this ring?" Faith asked.

Lindsey's tears dried. She leaned back in her chair and pursed her lips, staring pensively at the ring.

"You need to be honest right now," Faith replied. "We read through your court transcripts. You narrowly escaped being sentenced to a very long stint in prison. There's still time for that prison sentence to occur."

Lindsey looked over the agents' shoulders and stared petulantly at the wall. She looked like a spoiled child who had been told to take her hand out of the cookie jar, and Faith's brief sympathy faded.

"Mrs. Murray?" she asked, an edge coming to her voice. "Think of your children and answer my question. Who gave your husband this ring?"

Lindsey sighed and closed her eyes. Faith could see fresh tears forming, but they didn't fall this time. "It was his friend Peter."

Faith's heart leapt, but she kept her reaction under control. "Does Peter have a last name?"

"Olivera," Lindsey said. "He and Geoff were business partners. Geoff helped Peter get his position with Olive Branch International."

Michael and Faith widened their eyes in shock.

"Olive Branch International?" Michael exclaimed. "The peace organization?"

"One and the same," Lindsey replied, more than a trace of irony in her voice. "Peter was one of Geoff's silent partners when he started out in the black market. Peter was always worried about his reputations suffering if anyone found out, so he started to work for Olive Branch to establish how firmly anti-war he was. He took an awful lot of Geoff's money for someone who hated violence so much."

"Would he have wanted your husband dead? Say, if his name came up in an FBI probe?"

"It would be an ATF probe, not an FBI probe," Lindsey corrected with a touch of pettiness, "but Peter would have put his reputation ahead of anything else. He swears up and down that he had nothing to do with it." She smiled contemptuously. "But you can't trust a thief, can you?"

# CHAPTER EIGHT

Peter Olivera, like Lindsey Murray, lived on the outskirts of town, but this time, it was Pembroke, not Miller. On the thirty-minute drive to his place, Faith looked him up. "So it looks like our Mr. Olivera was an influential figure in Olive Branch. He was the figurehead of the Free Haiti movement of three years ago. Time magazine did a blurb on him in their One Hundred Faces of Freedom tribute the following year."

Michael whistled. "Damn. I'm guessing Murray's death changed all that."

"No. This is where it gets interesting. Olivera's connection to Murray was uncovered prior to Murray's death, *but*, not prior to the first rumors of Murray's activities in arms trafficking. There's a picture of the two of them talking and laughing together like old friends. When that came out, a lot of questions were raised about Olivera's association with a man suspected of trafficking weapons illegally."

"Maybe he killed Murray for revenge?"

"Maybe," Faith said.

"But why Jones?"

"Let's hope we get an answer to that as well," Faith said.

They pulled to a stop in front of a small, two-story plank cabin with a sharply angled roof and a stovepipe chimney. The cabin looked like the lair of a cartoon villain. The proportions seemed to be off, and the parts of the house that were clean were painted gunmetal grey, an odd and incongruous choice. Faith half-expected a crow with big round eyes and an oversized beak to stick its head out of the round second-floor window and caw at them raucously.

The laws of physics remained as they were, however, and when they knocked on the door, it was a very nervous middle-aged man who answered, not a warlock in flowing black robes.

Peter Olivera, like Lindsey Murray, looked much the worse for wear from his association with Murray. His ID said he was only fifty years old, but what little hair remained on his head was paper-white, and liver spots pockmarked his scalp. He had wrinkled hands and a lined face, and when he saw the FBI uniforms, he paled and nearly closed the door on them, only leaving it open when Turk growled.

"What is this?" he asked. "I've cooperated fully with law enforcement. You guys are supposed to warn me twenty-four hours before you arrive if you're coming to inspect anything."

"We're here to investigate the murders of Geoff Murray and Barrett James," Faith replied. "May we come in?"

"N—no," he said, trying once more to push the door closed.

Michael reached over Faith and put his hand on it, easily holding it open against the smaller man's feeble efforts. "Mr. Olivera?" Michael said, "if you have something to say, you want to say it now and not when we come back with a search warrant *and* an arrest warrant."

Peter paled a shade further, but slumped and acquiesced, allowing the agents to enter. "L-look," he said, "I know that you're here because I was an uh… associate… of Geoff's."

"Wife says you're a friend," Michael said, looking around the inside of the cabin, which, like Lindsey's house, was modestly appointed. Unlike Lindsey's house, which bore the signs that young children lived there, this cabin was impeccably organized and nearly spotless. Peter had evidently found a productive outlet for his anxiety.

"I was… look, it was just business, okay? I was trying to do good! So was Geoff, in his own way. Was he right? No. Was he a bad person? No. He was just misguided."

"What are you?" Faith asked, taking a seat on Peter's sofa and meeting his eyes.

"Well," Peter said, carefully lowering himself into an easy chair across from the sofa, "I was… driven. Is your dog housetrained?"

Turk looked up from his inspection and cast Peter an offended look.

"He's fine," Faith said, "he's helping us determine if you're the man who murdered Geoff Murray and Barret Jones."

Peter jumped, coming completely out of his chair and falling back down. "What? *Me?"* His voice was almost shrill.

"You were an *associate* of Murray's," Faith said, emphasizing Peter's word. "Your reputation took a nosedive when that came to light. You must have been upset at him."

"I wasn't upset at Geoff," Murray replied. "I'm upset at the world for just assuming we're assholes."

"Imagine thinking that it's a bad thing to sell weapons to terrorists," Michael said drily.

"Who are we to say that they don't have a right to fight for what they believe in?" Peter challenged, echoing Lindsey's words. "And besides, that was Geoff's angle, not mine. I was helping *end* wars!

Geoff always joked I would put him out of business. But he wasn't against it. In fact, he was for it. He was trying to put the right people in power, and I was trying to motivate the people that were in power to change their policies. We aren't warmongers, Special Agent. We're agents of peace. *Were* anyway."

*Sure,* Faith thought drily. *While we're talking, let me hear about that bridge you're trying to sell.* Hilarious as Peter's attempts at defending himself were, Faith wasn't here for him.

"We're not here to judge you, Mr. Olivera," Faith said. "We're here to find the man who murdered Barrett Jones. We know your connection to Mr. Murray. Did you know Barrett Jones?"

His eyes shifted to the left, and Faith said, "This would be a bad time to lie to us, Mr. Olivera."

Peter sighed. "Yes, I know Barrett. He and Geoff got into it a few years ago. Geoff showed up to a military reunion in his old Marine uniform, and Barrett kicked him out. Said Geoff dishonored the Corps by selling to terrorists or something. Things got heated, and Geoff ended up throwing a punch. I don't know what happened after that, but Geoff ended up leaving and burning his uniform. That's what he told me, anyway."

Faith and Michael shared a look. "And that was the only interaction the two of them had?"

"To my knowledge, yes."

"So where do you come in?"

Peter sighed. "I… convinced Barrett to let the assault go."

"I don't like that hesitation," Michael said. "What do you mean by 'convinced.'"

Peter ran his hands through his hair. "Jones received monthly benefits from Olive Branch. He qualified for the Heroes' Heart program where soldiers who had suffered PTSD as a result of their combat experience were entitled to health benefits along with their families through one of our contributing health providers. I…" he sighed and slumped. "I told him that if he wanted to keep his benefits, he needed to forget what had happened at the party."

"What a gentleman," Michael said contemptuously. "So you blackmailed him."

"I thought you said you weren't here to judge," Peter said petulantly.

"See, here's the problem," Michael said, shifting forward in his chair. "We now have a good motive for you to have killed Geoff

Murray and Barrett Jones. You knew both of them, and both of them, at one point, were a threat to you. Geoff's threat actually followed through. I imagine you had to work very hard to build your reputation and your life. To have that all taken from you? It's enough to piss anyone off."

"I didn't kill Geoff," Peter said stonily, "and I didn't kill Barrett. I have security footage to prove that I was here all night two nights ago. I wasn't even in town when Geoff died."

"Of course not," Faith said. "A man like you? You wouldn't get your own hands dirty. You'd pay someone else to do it."

Peter laughed. "Now you're just being ridiculous."

"Maybe," Faith said, "but I've seen a lot of ridiculous things. Look, I know it wasn't you who killed them. Your hands shake too much. Our killer would have needed steady hands to cut the victims the way he did."

Peter frowned, and there was not a trace of fear, knowledge or guilt in his reply. "Cut? Cut how?"

Faith hid her disappointment and said, "Both victims were cut from their wrists to their shoulders and across their throats. The cuts were surgical and completely uniform."

"Jesus," Peter said, "the news story didn't mention any of that."

"They wouldn't be allowed to," Faith said, "not in the middle of an ongoing criminal investigation."

"So let's say for the sake of argument that you're telling the truth," Michael said, "and you didn't kill Murray or Jones or have them killed. Any idea who might want to do that?"

"I don't know Jones well," Peter replied, "but if his temper is as abrasive as it seemed during our brief connection, I would say he probably angered someone who acted out of impulse."

*Oh no,* Faith thought. *Definitely not impulse.*

"As far as Geoff… well, you don't sell weapons for a living and make a lot of friends. He and I were probably the closest thing the other has to a friend."

"That doesn't quite answer my question," Faith pointed out.

Peter sighed. "I wish I could help you. Believe me. I've been living in fear, waiting for the day when whoever this guy is comes back for me and writes vengeance in my blood. Getting him off of the street is the best thing that could possibly happen to me.

"But I can't help you make that happen. The people I know for sure would have wanted Geoff gone would have hired a professional to do a professional hit. They wouldn't have paid some showboater to leave a signature like he's Jack the Ripper."

"Who would you have hired?"

Peter glared. "Check my financial records. See if you can find any large sums that didn't go to the DOJ or the FTC. I didn't hire anyone to kill Geoff, and for God's sake, I barely knew Barrett Jones. Why would I suddenly decide, after a year of peace, to murder a former Marine and risk losing what little life I have left?" He looked around his cabin and said, "I like it here. It's peaceful. It's quiet. It's just enough for me. I would do anything to keep it. I wouldn't kill someone. If you don't believe I wouldn't do it because it's morally wrong, believe I wouldn't do it because I know if I did, I would get caught and end up serving that prison sentence I spent over five hundred million dollars avoiding."

That, Faith could believe.

"Can you tell me what unit Geoff was a part of?"

"He was a cook. I don't know what unit. He was a cook, but he was proud to be a Marine. At least until Barrett called him on it.

Faith looked at Turk, who had finished snooping and now sat next to her. He shook his head in a surprisingly human gesture, and Faith sighed inwardly.

She stood and nodded at Peter. "Thank you for your time. We'll reach out if we have any further questions."

"You do that," Peter said.

"Don't leave town," Michael warned.

"Where would I go?" Peter replied.

The sun had set by the time they left Peter's house. Michael switched on the high beams, and the lights cut an eerie swath into the landscape. The lights of Pembroke glowed like a nightlight ahead, adding rather than subtracting to the sense of otherworldliness.

This was what Barrett Jones would have seen during his last few moments on Earth. Would he have feared the dark and the calm, or would the solitude have brought him some solace in his last moments?

She hoped for the latter. All Marines accepted that they might leave the suck on their shield instead of with it, but Jones hadn't gone out that way. He had served his country well and been taken from it not by an enemy but by the most malicious of friendly fire.

She reached down to stroke Turk's fur. *We'll get 'em, Owl*, she thought. *We'll get the assholes that did this to you.*

# CHAPTER NINE

*Faith was bound this time, and when she tested the bonds, they held fast. She could speak, though. She was as she was when she really was tortured.*

*And she could feel pain.*

*She knew this because when the knife sliced under her knee, the same shocking, brilliant bolt of pain shot through her leg that shot through her when Trammell actually cut her shot through her again. Just as she had twenty-seven months ago, she screamed.*

*"I almost had him that time, didn't I, Faith?" a voice spoke.*

*It wasn't Trammell who spoke this time, though, but West. Franklin West, the Copycat Donkey Killer who had become nearly five times as prolific as the original Donkey Killer and professed to be twice that prolific, a claim Faith was inclined to think was true.*

*Trammell reached around her with the knife and sliced the tendon at the top of her knee. She shrieked again as her quadricep muscled bunched tightly and painfully in her upper thigh.*

*"Careful, Jethro," West warned. "You'll slice her femoral artery, and then she'll wake up."*

*"I'll be careful," Jethro promised. "I know what I'm doing."*

*"You..." Faith hissed through gritted teeth. "Assholes."*

*Trammell sliced through the underside of her other knee, and Faith cried out again. Her body began to shake, and she knew that a few deep cuts later, she would pass out from the pain.*

*It wasn't the deep cuts that worried her. It was the little cuts that came in between. Trammell would slice her upper knee open, then leave her like that for a half hour while he sliced at her arms and shoulders little by little. Then, he would sever both of her Achilles' tendons and she would finally pass out, moments before Michael burst in and shot Trammell just before he sliced her throat.*

*"There's no need to be rude," West said. "When you die, you get to wake up and forget all about what's happening now. I get to wake up living with my failure to kill Turk. I'm not used to failure, Faith. It bothers me. It eats at me terribly. Does that make you happy?"*

*Faith grinned. "I told you. I'm going to catch you, West. I* will *bring you to justice."*

*"Maybe," West said, "but not if you keep wasting your time on cases like this one."*

*"Why would I waste my time on a dead man and a man on the run?"*

*Jethro severed her left quadricep from her knee, and Faith gasped as a fresh shock of pain coursed through her, ending in more shaking and a wave of nausea. She wouldn't vomit, she knew, but the nausea would flare up with each cut.*

*"That's a good point," Jethro said in his incongruously high-pitched tenor voice. "I don't even get to wake up at all."*

*"That's because Michael Prince beat you," West said. "He rescued Faith before you had a chance to kill her."*

*"She really is lucky, isn't she?"*

*Faith laughed in spite of the pain she felt. If her subconscious was trying to convince her that she still resented Michael for rescuing her, then she was wasting her own time. "We're partners," she reminded them—herself, really. "There's no shame in being rescued by someone whose job is to have your back."*

*"I don't think that's what you're ashamed of, Faith," West said. "I think you just don't like to lose. This is all just a game to you. The reason you're obsessed with me—and let's be honest, the person you're really obsessed with is the dead man torturing your soul right now—is because Jethro beat you. Then I wore his costume and beat you again."*

*Jethro sliced through her right Achilles tendon. It was not the act she expected and differed from what had really happened. The shock made the pain a thousand times worse, and Faith cried out in anguish.*

*"I wonder," West continued do you ever consider things from the perspective of your killers? I don't mean surface questions like why they killed their victims or why they chose this method or that method. I mean, have you ever* really *tried to think like they do? Like* we *do?"*

*Trammell sliced her other Achilles heel, but once more reality differed. She didn't pass out or wake up, and when she tried to close her eyes and force herself away, her eyelids wouldn't move. Whatever limited control she had earlier, she didn't have it anymore.*

*"I did," West said. "I studied you extensively. I learned everything I possibly could about you. I learned your past and your present and as much as I could about your future. I learned your habits, studied your mannerisms, tried to walk a mile in your shoes, then ten more miles. I*

*bonded with you, Faith. I laughed with you, cried with you, cheered with you, shouted with you. I was as close with you as any husband."*

*Faith chuckled at that in spite of her pain.*

*"I was," West insisted. "Not in terms of physical intimacy, of course, but in terms of emotional and intellectual intimacy. Be honest, Faith. Be perfectly honest. I was a good therapist, wasn't I?"*

*Faith met his eyes. "You were. You gave me the strength to beat you."*

*"I gave you the strength to fight back, Faith. I still intend to beat you. But you don't know why. You know the reason I gave you, but you don't know the real reason. I know you, but you don't know me."*

*Faith thought about it. The last time she'd dreamed of West and Trammell together, the dream had been her subconscious trying to tell her something. She believed the same thing was happening now.*

*"Time to wake up, Faith," West said.*

*Jethro leaned over her, and for the first time in this dream, Faith saw his bright blue eyes, his crazed, wide grin. She could smell his sour breath, and her nostrils flared as he leaned close and said, "Let's see how you bleed, little girl."*

*His smile disappeared in a mask of pure, unbridled rage. He pressed the knife to her throat and drew it across.*

Faith sat upright, gasping and shaking. Turk jumped onto the bed next to her side and immediately began licking her until she found enough presence of mind to gently push him away and say, "I'm okay, Turk. I'm okay."

Michael was on the phone. His stiff shoulders and thinly pressed lips under dejected eyes told Faith exactly what he was hearing.

"Thank you," he said. "We're on our way."

He hung up and sighed. "Well," he said. "I don't know how much you heard, but I think you can figure it out."

"Another victim."

"What else?"

Faith's shoulders sagged. Dammit, she knew this was going to happen. Would it be so bad if she were wrong about this just once?

She shook off her disappointment and adopted a professional demeanor. "All right. Let's head to the scene."

***

"Gabriel Duke," Michael said, "Lobbyist for the Big Five defense contractors."

"All five?" Faith asked. "They wouldn't want their competitors to struggle?"

"Not at the government's hands," Michael said. "If the government made life hard for one of them, that would make life hard for all of them."

Faith turned back to their body. "Life got pretty hard for Gabriel Duke."

Duke lay spread eagle on the ground in a dirt lot once owned by a defunct construction company and now owned by the Washington State Department of Natural Resources. The cause of death was the same as the other two victims, and the cuts on his arms and throat were also identical. The word vengeance was written a little higher than with the previous victims. This was probably because, unlike them, he hadn't been moved after death.

"What was he doing here?" Faith asked. "In the middle of nowhere, by himself?"

"According to the DNR, he was negotiating a purchase of this lot to convert into office space for his lobbying company. He wanted to relocate to Central Washington so he and his wife could lead a quieter life. Guess that didn't work out for him."

Turk stepped forward and sniffed at the body, then trotted past to search for clues. Faith folded her arms and thought. A former Marine, an arms dealer and a lobby for defense contractors. Their killer was definitely looking for people involved with the military.

But why these victims? Why them specifically? There had to be a reason beyond their vague connection to defense.

In her nightmare, the image of Doctor West told her that she needed to think like a criminal to answer those questions. So how did her criminal think?

Well, one thing was clear. He wanted vengeance.

Vengeance. Not justice. Not right. Vengeance. Somehow or other, their killer knew all of these three victims personally, *intimately*, as Dream West had said. He was getting them back for a wrong done to him, a wrong he felt heinous enough to warrant death.

"We're still looking for someone who knew all three of them," she said. "Someone wanted them dead specifically, and for a specific reason."

"What reason?" Michael asked. "That's what we need to know. We find that, we find our killer."

"Agreed," Faith said. "How soon until CSI gets here?"

"Probably about five minutes before Turk finished doing their job for them," Michael quipped.

Faith chuckled and said, "Well, in the meantime, let's see if we can find anything helpful."

"I'll check the body," Michael said, stooping down and pulling gloves from his jacket pocket.

"Got a hunch?" Faith asked.

"No. I just don't feel like walking around in this cold."

Faith smiled. "If you're cold, walking around will warm you up."

"There's other things that'll warm me up, if you're offering," Michael said. He reddened and immediately added, "I didn't mean that. Bad joke. Sorry."

In the past, she and Michael had dated, but both agreed to end it and decided to remain friends. Now Faith was with David, and Michael was with his new wife, Ellie, so the jokes they used to tell each other were a little more awkward now. Faith was glad it was Michael and not herself who had to bear the brunt of the awkwardness this time.

"It's all right," Faith said. "I'll just make sure to tell Ellie exactly what you said."

Michael rolled his eyes. "You're a true friend, Faith."

Faith walked to Turk, who was sniffing around for any sign of the killer's tracks. She was sure Turk would find anything long before she did, so instead of digging for clues, she continued to try to put herself in her victims' headspace.

Why kill them like this? Why slit their hands and throats after death and write vengeance above their heads? The word was clear, but why the ritual of cutting them?

The heart was the first cut, the killing blow. Then after killing them, the killer sliced the "river of life" veins in the forearms and the brachial arteries. Then he severed both jugulars and carotids. He killed the heart, which was hidden, then severed the major visible blood vessels of the body.

The inside died, then the outside. Or the inside was already dead, and that exposed the rot of the outside. Or he just needed them to be still while he cut them, and piercing their heart was the easiest way to do that.

She sighed and folded her arms again. She wished she had paid more attention in her FBI profiling classes. A friend of hers in the Academy was training to join the Behavioral Analysis Unit and had tried to convince Faith to join her, but Faith preferred field work. She liked catching and stopping bad guys, not trying to psychoanalyze them.

If she had focused more on that, could she have caught West sooner? Could she have made better decisions when she was hunting Trammell? Would any of that have mattered, or would she have been unable to resist her desire to be the face they saw when justice finally found them?

"Faith!" Michael called. "I've got something!"

Faith left that speculation aside and rushed to the body, Turk at her side. Michael showed her a slip of paper. "Found this in Duke's pocket."

Faith took the paper. A phone number was written in glittering pink ink, and underneath the number was the address where they now stood and a time: eleven-thirty p.m.

"I guess he wasn't here for the land," Faith said.

"Guess not," Michael agreed.

"Well," Faith said, "Let's go have a chat with the owner of this phone number."

## CHAPTER TEN

The owner of the phone number turned out to be none other than Gabriel Duke's personal assistant. Despite a long and by outward appearances happy twenty-year marriage with his wife, Susanne, Gabriel Duke had apparently enjoyed an ongoing tryst with his personal assistant, Henry Faulks.

The phone number yielded an address at an extended stay hotel in the nearby city of Westhaven, the seat of the county where Miller and Pembroke resided. It was a forty-minute drive to the hotel, and while they drove, Faith looked up Henry Faulks.

She found quite a few interesting things about him. In addition to being Gabriel Duke's assistant for the past ten years, he was a Marine combat veteran, a tank gunner and loader assigned to the ninth mechanized brigade. He had met Barrett Jones at a convention, and according to a complaint filed by Jones with the Portland Police Department, he had become violent when Jones refused his advances. Jones, apparently, had quite easily handled Faulks and held him until the Military Police arrived.

She imagined that Faulks would have found that rather humiliating. Possibly enough to kill Jones, but the interesting facts didn't end there. He had also gotten into a violent confrontation with Geoff Murray, when the latter had accused his boss and secret lover of being fully aware of illegal arms trafficking and picking and choosing who got to work and who got prosecuted based on who bribed him the most.

That altercation had landed him in jail for assault for a month. Somehow, he had kept his job with Duke.

Well, not somehow. Faith knew exactly how.

They arrived at the extended stay just as the sun left the eastern horizon behind and began to ascend skyward. The motel looked like any other similar place, though perhaps a little cleaner than usual. Faith wondered why Duke hadn't let his lover and assistant stay at least in the same hotel. It would be easy enough to explain that away by saying that he needed the man at his beck and call. In fact, making him stay in an extended stay a forty-minute drive from Pembroke was more suspicious than renting him a room at the same hotel.

Unless, of course, things were no longer so rosy between the two of them.

The agents walked into the lobby looking to get Henry's room number, but when they walked inside, they saw him in the lobby drinking coffee and chatting with the concierge. He looked up at them, and when his eyes saw the FBI uniforms, his smile vanished.

He looked up at Faith, and before Faith could say anything, he ran, tossing the coffee cup behind him at the agents. The concierge cried out, but the cup and the hot liquid it contained landed well ahead of the three and did no damage.

The agents immediately rushed after Henry. "Henry Faulks!" Faith shouted. "Stop!"

Turk rushed ahead and quickly caught up to Henry, but Henry landed a well-aimed kick, sending Turk sprawling, and turned down a hallway. Faith's blood boiled. She had had enough of telling people not to hurt her dog.

She rounded the corner and sped past Michael, adrenaline forcing her ever faster. Turk still easily outpaced her but was once more foiled when Henry reached a door and slammed it closed into the dog's face. Turk barked and threw himself into the door, nearly knocking Henry over, but Henry steadied himself, shifted his stance and pushed the door shut.

"Fuck off!" Henry shrieked. He stared at the agents and tried to glare, but his pale face and terrified eyes made the attempt pathetic.

Hell, the whole situation was pathetic.

"Henry," Faith said patiently. "You know we're going to get out there. Save yourself some embarrassment and just open the door."

"No!" he cried. "Your dog's going to kill me!"

"So let's make a deal," Faith said. "You put your hands on your head, take three steps back, get on your knees and cross your ankles behind you, and I'll tell Turk not to attack you. He'll listen to me."

Henry looked at Turk, who continued to snarl at him.

"Turk, hold," Faith commanded.

Turk looked at Faith and immediately backed off, keeping his eyes on Henry but no longer barking.

"See?" Faith said. "He'll behave. Now it's your turn."

Instead of complying, Henry turned and sprinted toward a car parked in the first row of spaces on the side of the hotel. Faith rolled her eyes and said, "All right. Take him down, Turk."

She opened the door and Turk barreled after Henry, catching him just as he opened the door to a late model BMW and dragging him to the ground. Henry shrieked and brought his fist down over and over on Turk's head, but the blows were weak and didn't harm Turk in the slightest.

Faith and Michael walked over, and Faith knelt over Henry and looked down into his eyes. "Are you going to behave now?" she asked.

Henry sighed and nodded. "Yes. I'm sorry."

"Save the apologies for later," Faith said. "You might have to add a few."

***

Henry shivered uncontrollably in the conference room Faith and Michael had commandeered in the hotel to interrogate him. Faith had the heater on, but it wasn't discomfort—not physical discomfort, anyway—that caused the tremors.

"You want some water?" Michael asked. "Maybe some coffee? The decaf here is pretty good, or so I'm told."

Henry shook his head.

"I'll take a head shake for that answer and that answer only," Michael replied, "the rest are going to have to involve words. Got it?"

Henry nodded. Michael leaned forward and lifted his eyebrows, and Henry said, "Yes."

Faith was having Michael take the lead on this interrogation. She hoped that Michael would be able to intimidate him and make him think better of any lies he planned to tell.

"Perfect," Michael said, "We'll start with this: did you kill Gabriel Duke?"

Henry stared at Michael in disbelief. "Gabe's dead?"

Michael looked at Faith. Henry's shock seemed genuine, but if he didn't know Gabe was dead, then why run from them?

Michael thought the same thing, apparently. "New question: why did you run from us?"

"I thought…" Henry's eyes shifted to the left, and Michael caught it.

"No," he said, "no lying. We like you a lot for three murders right now, and lying won't help."

Henry glared at Michael. "Okay. I didn't kill anyone. Am I released? No? I guess the truth isn't helping me either."

Turk growled softly and Henry paled.

"Attitude won't help either," Michael said.

Henry sighed and said, "I don't know. I mean, Gabe is pissing off a lot of people in Washington right now. I thought that maybe someone found some dirt on him, and they were trying to get me to confirm it."

"What kind of dirt?" Michael asked.

Henry clammed up.

Michael smiled and lifted his hands just off of the table. "All right. We'll circle back to that. Yes, Gabriel Duke is dead. So are Barrett Jones and Geoff Murray."

Henry's eyes widened, and once more, Michael caught the body language. "Ah. We recognize these names, yes?"

"Yes, but… didn't Geoff Murray die like a year ago?"

"He did indeed," Michael confirmed. "Here's the thing. He died from a stab wound to the heart. After he died, he was moved, and his arms and throat were cut. Then someone wrote the word vengeance over his head in his own blood."

Faith watched Henry carefully, but he betrayed no sign that he recognized the description. He grimaced in disgust and said, "God, that's awful."

"I know, right?" Michael said. "What makes it worse is that he was killed during the week you and Duke were here to meet with representatives from RTX. And Barrett Jones and Gabriel Duke were murdered the same way, both dying after you got back here."

Henry paled further. "Oh God. He… he cut Gabe like that?"

"Yep," Michael said. "Gruesome scene."

Henry's lower lip trembled, and he lowered his head and began to weep softly. Michael glanced at Faith again.

His grief was real. Those weren't forced tears. But he was showing considerable guilt along with his fear. That could be as simple as the fact that he and Duke had argued recently, or it could be that he felt guilty for killing his lover.

Faith nodded at Michael, and Michael turned back to Henry and continued. "If this really wasn't you," he said, "then I'm sorry for your loss."

"It wasn't me," Henry insisted, his voice thick.

"See," Michael said, folding his hands on the table. "I want to believe you, but there are a lot of things that don't make sense, and a few things that really do make sense, and not in a good way. You knew all three victims, and you had reason to hate all three of them."

"Why the fuck would I hate Gabriel?" Henry said through his tears. "I…" He blinked, and his tears dried up as he realized what he was about to say.

"You loved him," Faith finished. "That doesn't mean you didn't kill him."

"I *didn't* kill him!"

"It must have pissed you off when he broke up with you," Michael said. "After all this time, all of those promises, to be discarded like that? Like you were nothing more than a toy. It must have really bothered you."

"Especially after you took care of that little Geoff Murray problem he had," Faith added.

"You guys are delusional!" Henry protested.

"Are we?" Michael asked. "Geoff Murray exposed your boss's dishonesty and jeopardized his career. Barrett Jones rejected your advances, and when you got petulant about it, he embarrassed you in front of a lot of people."

"Barrett is delusional too," Henry said. "I hit on him, yes, but I was respectful about it. All he had to do was politely decline, and I would have left him alone. Instead, he got all spazzy and shouted for me to keep my hands off of him—I didn't touch him, by the way—and called me all sorts of names. I'm sure you've heard them, so I won't repeat them. And *he* attacked *me*."

"Damn," Faith said, "that sounds like even more reason to kill him."

Henry blinked and reddened a little. "Well," he said lamely, "I didn't."

"Gabriel Duke used you, then tossed you aside. I'm going to go out on a limb and say that you really loved him. You thought that the two of you were going to have a future, and he threw you out like yesterday's garbage."

"No," Henry insisted emphatically, "I *never* thought we were going to have a future. Did I love him? Yes, but I didn't think we would ever have anything beyond fun and a few stolen moments. And it was only a few moments. We weren't sleeping together regularly, we just hooked up a few times. I didn't do that because I loved him, I did it because he was hot, and I like sex. Sorry to take away the lifetime movie fantasy, but I wasn't trash to him. I was an occasional tool for him to let off some steam, and that's all he was to me."

"But you loved him?"

"As a person. As a friend. As a leader. I was offended at Geoff's accusations because Geoff Murray was a slimeball who capitalized off of genocide. Gabe was a good man who advocated for a strong military because he knew that only through strength could we preserve peace."

"He got paid pretty well for that, didn't he?" Michael pointed out.

"It wasn't about money to Gabe!" Henry shouted. "Sure, he made money, but he could have made money any number of ways. He chose this job because he could make money *and* make a difference."

"Why did you ask him to meet you last night?" Faith asked.

Henry paled again. "I don't know what you're talking about."

Turk growled, and Henry flinched.

"Let's try that again," Michael said. "Why did you meet Gabe last night?"

"I didn't meet him!"

Faith pulled the paper Michael had found from her pocket. "So this isn't your handwriting and phone number?"

Henry paled further. He took a breath and said, "Okay, yes. I asked him to meet me. But I didn't show up."

"Why?"

"Because…" Henry's eyes shifted back and forth, and Turk growled again. "Goddammit, I get it!" Henry snapped at the dog.

Turk gave Faith a dry glance and Faith said, "You have to see things from our perspective, Henry. We have three victims, all of whom were murdered the same way when you were here in town, all of whom provided you with a motive."

"Gabriel didn't do anything. I had no desire to kill him. I didn't want to kill anyone."

"So tell us what happened," Michael prompted gently.

"For God's sake," Henry snapped. "That's not a confession. I didn't *accidentally* kill anyone either."

"Then why did you lure Gabriel out to that abandoned lot?"

"I didn't lure him out. I just…" he sighed and said, "something came up, and I couldn't meet him."

"Or cancel on him?"

"It was an emergency. I didn't think."

Faith and Michael looked at each other again. "You're asking us to believe a lot," Faith said, "on no evidence. Meanwhile, we have a growing pile of evidence that suggests that you were the one to kill these three men. Can you provide alibis for the previous night, three nights ago, and the night of Geoff Murray's murder? At this point, that's what you're going to need to avoid charges."

Henry looked between the two agents and sighed. "Fuck," he said heavily. "I… look, I have an alibi, but can I plead the fifth or something?"

"Do you understand what that means?"

"It means I can't incriminate myself. So if I say something, you guys can't use it against me."

"No," Michael said, not correct. What it means is that you can choose not to say something that would incriminate you. The catch-twenty-two is that if you do that, you'll essentially be admitting that you've done something criminal, and we *will* arrest you."

Henry looked between them and said, "I think I need a lawyer."

Faith looked at Michael, then at Henry. "We can get you a lawyer, but if we do that, we have to formally arrest you for these murders. You'll definitely be headed to an arraignment and then an indictment, and unless something comes up that completely clears your name, a trial."

Henry tapped the table with his finger and thought. "What if I make a deal?"

Faith looked at Michael again. "What kind of deal?" Michael asked.

"I can prove that I wasn't the person who killed Gabriel. If I do that, it saves you two a lot of time trying to put the wrong person in jail. In return, I want immunity."

"Not enough," Michael said, "not nearly enough. You need to give us something, not show us we have nothing."

"How about my partners?" Henry said. "I can give you the names of everyone else involved."

"Involved in what?"

"No." Henry shook his head. "Guarantee first, then I talk."

Faith leaned forward. "I guarantee you we find out everything whether you tell us or not, and when we find out, we make sure this is as hard on you as it possibly can be. How does that sound?"

Henry sighed, and his lip trembled again. "Goddammit."

"Sucks when the consequences of your actions catch up with you, doesn't it?"

He scoffed bitterly and said, "Look, can you at least make it so I don't end up in too rough a prison? I don't want to get hurt."

“We can suggest that you be housed in protective custody,” Faith said, “assuming that what you’re about to tell us is a prison-worthy offence. I’m guessing that’s a pretty good assumption.”

"Yeah," Henry said moodily. "It is." He sighed again and said, "All right. Well, it's better than murder anyway. I was involved in a narcotics ring. I am involved in it. Well, was involved until now."

"Was that what came up?" Faith asked, "That took you out of your meeting with Mr. Duke?"

“Yes,” he replied. “I was contacted by a partner of mine. His mules got caught at the Mexican border, and he needed advice on what to do next. He was afraid that the mules would connect him to the crime, so we had to make some phone calls and make sure that wouldn’t happen.” Seeing Faith and Michael’s expressions, he said, “by bribing officials, not by killing the mules! God, I’m not a murderer!”

“All right,” Faith said, “Start telling us everything.”

# CHAPTER ELEVEN

Faith and Michael watched the DEA agents take Henry Faulks from the interrogation room. He had confessed to being one of the principles in a large drug ring that shipped heroin and marijuana from Mexico and distributed it to most of the Midwest. Henry named several high-ranking government officials as co-conspirators, but Faith and Michael were going to let the DEA take credit for that.

This was a win for justice, but a loss for the three FBI agents, and not because of the credit they wouldn't receive. Once more, a promising lead had turned out to be nothing important, and once more, they were back to square one.

"It's crazy," Michael said. "I've never seen so many suspects with so many great motives turn out to be dead ends. Two of them were even criminals, three if you count Murray's widow." He shook his head. "It's just insane."

"That's what's making this difficult," Faith agreed. "We're not trying to find the one guy who fits the murderer's profile, we're trying to figure out which of the many people who fit actually did the deeds. We're not trying to find a needle in a haystack, we're trying to find a needle in a stack of needles."

Michael looked out the window, where the sky had gone dark. Getting Henry's statement and waiting for the DEA to arrive to transport him had taken the day from them.

Faith checked the time. It was late, but not so late they couldn't keep working. "I want to talk to Duke's wife," Faith said. "PD should have notified her about her husband's death by now."

Henry had explained that he was in a different hotel because Duke was in town with his wife. Susanne knew about them, he said, but obviously drew the line at sleeping in the same bed where the two got it on. That was why Duke would visit Henry and not the other way around.

"Works for me," Michael said.

The three of them headed to the hotel where Duke was staying. The concierge greeted them with the typical plastic smile that every customer service professional wore. “Good evening. I can get you a room, but I’m afraid we’re not pet-friendly.”

“He’s an FBI K9 unit,” Faith corrected, “not a pet. We’re here to speak to Susanne Duke. Can you give us her room number, please?”

“No, I’m afraid not,” the concierge replied. “We don’t disclose that information.”

Faith stared at her a moment. “You realize we’re FBI, right?”

“I realize that you’re wearing vests with the letters FBI on them,” the concierge replied.

Her tone and expression remained professional, but it was clear she didn’t believe they were really FBI. Faith sighed and said, “All right. Would you like to verify our IDs?”

“I would, thank you.”

Faith and Michael handed over their IDs. “You can wait over there while I verify these,” the concierge said.

“We’ll wait here, thank you.”

Irritation flashed across the woman’s face. “I have other guests waiting—”

“They’ll wait,” Faith snapped. “Verify those IDs and give us Susanne Duke’s room number.”

The concierge’s smile faded. She looked up the IDs, her lips thin. When she confirmed that she was, in fact, making things difficult for sworn FBI agents, she gasped. “Oh,” she said meekly. “I’m so sorry.”

Faith didn’t really care. “Room number.”

"Two-fifty-seven. I'm so sorry—"

“Thank you.”

Room two-fifty-seven was, strangely enough, on the first floor rather than the second. Faith knocked on the door, and a beautiful middle-aged woman with a statuesque figure and long blonde hair answered. When she saw the FBI uniforms, her eyes widened. “Oh my,” she said, “what was Gabriel into?”

Faith and Michael exchanged a look. Susanne Duke was showing no sign of grief at her husband’s death. Faith turned back to Susanne and said, “Good evening, ma’am. My name is Faith Bold. I’m a special agent with the FBI. This is my partner, Special Agent Michael Prince, and my K9 unit Turk. Have the police contacted you regarding your husband?”

“They told me he was murdered. I identified his body earlier today.”

Faith and Michael shared another look.

“Would you like to come in?” Susanne asked.

“Thank you,” Faith said. “We’ll try to keep this brief.”

Susanne led them inside and gestured to the sofa. “You can sit there if you’d like. Would you like coffee? Gabriel brought some heirloom stuff from Kenya with him. I couldn’t tell you the difference between this and burnt charcoal, but he swore that it was the most delicious coffee he’d ever tasted.”

“I’ll take some,” Michael said. “Thank you.”

Faith suppressed the urge to roll his eyes. Michael was like a kid with candy when it came to coffee. “I’m all right, thank you,” Faith said.

Susanne shrugged. “Suit yourself. I won’t have any either. I’m more of a kombucha person.”

She started the coffee and as she measured the water and the grounds, she said, “If you’re wondering why I’m not weeping with grief, it’s because Gabriel and I hadn’t been in love for a very long time. I’m not happy that he’s dead, but I’m not exactly broken up over it.” She turned to the agents and added, “The security footage will prove that I couldn’t have killed him either. I was here last night. All night.”

“And you didn’t think to wonder why Gabriel left the hotel early?”

Susanne scoffed. “No, I didn’t wonder. I knew exactly where he was going.” She started the coffee maker and fetched a mug from a cabinet in the kitchen. “My husband had numerous affairs, Special Agent, men and women. He wasn’t one to limit himself sexually. I learned very early on that I would never be the only one.”

“So you believed your husband was meeting a lover?”

“Henry, yes,” Susanne said. “Those two were off and on ever since Gabriel hired him. I never liked Henry. He was prone to fits of anger that were truly terrifying. It wouldn’t surprise me to learn that he killed Gabriel.”

“We’ve already ruled him out as a suspect,” Faith said.

“Really? Now that *is* surprising. I told Gabriel to leave him and find someone else to play with. I had a hunch that Henry was going to do something violent someday. He was always so angry. But Gabriel never listened. He always thought he knew better.”

She poured coffee into Michael's mug and handed it to him. He sipped it, and his eyes widened in appreciation. Susanne smiles slightly, and her eyes traveled up and down Michael as he savored the coffee.

Faith had a feeling that Susanne had enjoyed her own dalliances when she and Gabriel were married.

She confirmed it a moment later when she said, "I had my fun too, of course. He and I had a heart-to-heart about five years after we married, and I told him that I didn't love him anymore, but I enjoyed the lifestyle he was able to provide me. I told him that I knew he didn't love me either but needed me for his career. We agreed to stay married and keep our dirty laundry hidden, but neither of us expected more than that from each other. I didn't sleep around nearly as much as Gabriel did—caution was a word that meant little to him—but I can't claim that I was deprived."

She sat in the easy chair across from the sofa and crossed her legs, her eyes still on Michael. "There's something exciting about infidelity, even if what we had wasn't strictly infidelity. What do you think, Prince?"

Michael frowned. "I think I'm not here to talk about your love life. I'd like to know who you think might have killed Gabriel."

"Well, I thought Henry killed him," she said, not seeming to be bothered by Michael shutting her down, "but you're telling me he didn't. So now I'm not sure what to think."

"Did he have conflict with anyone else?" Faith asked.

Susanne laughed. "Special Agent, he was a lobbyist. It was his job to piss people off. I'll bet you anything there are half a dozen hitmen scrambling to claim that they were the one who finally killed him."

Faith was getting tired of Susanne's ego. She acted like she was the star of her own little movie. If there was one thing all of their suspects had in common, it was that they were all self-centered. Susanne's smirk reminded her of West's smug smile, and she leaned forward and looked coldly at the woman. "Mrs. Duke, someone murdered your husband last night. Maybe that doesn't matter to you, but it does to us. This person also murdered a known arms dealer, and while that might not be much loss to society, he also killed an innocent Marine two nights before that, an innocent Marine who was on his way home to his wife and young children. I don't give a rat's ass about your little soap opera life. I need to figure out who's killing people and stop them before more innocent people die. So if you have any information that can help me and maybe incline me to refrain from airing that dirty laundry you've kept so hidden to every news network I can look up, now would be an excellent time to provide it."

Michael looked at Faith and frowned. Faith felt a touch of guilt for threatening Susanne like that. Susanne might be a piece of work, but that didn't justify coercion.

Her anger outweighed her guilt, though, and she felt a surge of satisfaction when Susanne paled a shade. The older woman covered it well, years of being in the spotlight affording her a practiced gravitas. She shrugged and said, "If Henry wasn't the killer, the only person I could think of is Guthrie Henderson. He was a PR manager for a smaller defense firm that was trying to break into the industry. They hired Gabriel to advocate for their product in Washington. Gabriel accepted the job, but a larger competitor made him a better offer, so he discontinues his relationship with them and took the better offer. Guthrie became irate and claimed my husband was a traitor and a backstabber, yadda yadda. It nearly came to blows, but security stepped in."

"How long ago was this?"

"Nearly two years ago," Susanne said.

"Have you heard anything from Henderson since?"

"Yes," Susanne said, "the business went bankrupt last month. Guthrie left a long drunken message claiming that he hoped to see my husband in hell someday and this, that and the other. I didn't take it seriously, but now that Gabriel is dead and Henry is apparently not the killer, I'm wondering if Henderson decided to carry out his threat since he has nothing left to lose. Also, the company is based in Yakima, about two hours west."

"Do you have Henderson's contact information?"

"I have his old work contact information," Susanne said, "but I don't know if they still work. He called my husband from a hotel landline."

"We'll give it a shot," Faith replied. "Thank you."

She was happy to leave the older woman behind. Michael seemed just as relieved, though for a different reason. "Christ, do wedding rings mean nothing to people?" he groused.

"They don't seem to mean much to her," Faith said.

"Good point." Michael looked up at the sky, which had gone completely dark now. The moon was new, and the canopy of stars above was breathtaking.

But their minds weren't on the view. Faith looked up Henderson's company. They were still operating despite going through bankruptcy. Faith looked up directions and found that it would take exactly two hours to get from their hotel to the company. “We’ll leave tomorrow morning at seven a.m.,” she said, “and see what Mr. Henderson has to say for himself.”

# CHAPTER TWELVE

Doc carefully buffed the scalpel to a gleaming shine and set it on the tray next to his other instruments. He smiled lovingly at the tools for a while before tidying his workspace and washing his hands. He carefully packed the instruments away and set them back in his messenger bag. The bag was a gift, one of the few he kept from his old life, not because it held any emotional significance for him but because it was actually very useful.

He stood from the work bench and walked over to the display case he kept in the opposite corner of the room. He stood, hands clasped behind his back in parade rest, and looked at the mementos he had taken, reminders of those who had laid down their lives for the purpose of justice.

The wristwatch was the newest. He took that off of Gabriel Duke. It was a Rolex, an expensive model, one of their nautical pieces with a compass and smaller dials in the face that told the month and date. Doc couldn't understand people's fascination with wristwatches. No wristwatch on earth was as accurate as the cheapest cell phone. They were pretty, to be sure. He could understand owning one as a piece of art, but he couldn't understand carrying it around as though it were a tool. He supposed Duke must have thought of it as jewelry, the way a woman might see a pearl necklace.

The cigarette lighter belonged to Geoff Murray. It was almost as garish as the watch, made of gold with a diamond-encrusted engraving of Murray's initials. Doc shook his head. The lighter's purpose was to ignite paper rolls filled with dried tobacco. It, at least, was a tool, but you could get the same result from a two-dollar piece at a gas station. Once more, it seemed foolish for anyone to carry such a monstrosity.

The purple heart was from Barrett Jones, something Jones kept in his breast pocket and told no one, not even his wife, about. He picked it up and ran his fingers lightly over the medal. Of all the pieces in his collection, this one was the only one that had any real meaning, any deep meaning. He could understand why Barrett carried this, even though it held no practical use and was a rather cheap construction of polished brass and silk ribbon. Silk was a nice material but not very expensive these days.

In dollar amount, it was the least valuable of his collection. In meaning, it was the most valuable.

He hated it.

His fist closed around it, and he had to will himself not to squeeze so tightly that he cut through the glove and got his oils or skin cells on the medal.

He set the medal carefully in its place and glared at it. Wounded in the act of murdering other people. And the country celebrated it. Like Barrett was some kind of hero because he got shot by someone he was trying to kill. *How dare those people defend themselves?* he thought with bitter sarcasm. What pieces of shit they must be.

He took a breath and released it slowly, calming slightly as he did.

Barrett was dead. He had paid for his crimes. So had Duke. So had Murray. So had everyone whose lives were memorialized in this case. A handkerchief from a former General who had ordered the massacre of a group of insurgents fighting to take their homeland back. A photograph of a man who had paid a third-world country to start a war with their neighbor so he could sell medical kits to the United Nations when they started their inevitable humanitarian mission. A newspaper clipping from the hometown paper of a Corporal who liked taking headshots because he liked the way their heads exploded.

He was the only one of Doc's targets who Doc had killed form a distance, shooting him with an air rifle from a hundred yards away. His head hadn't exploded, but he had died all the same. Doc hadn't anticipated the Corporal's truck hitting a tree, nor had he anticipated that the Corporal's blood alcohol content would be four times the legal limit, but that was all right. He didn't need to mark all of his victims. Only those whose crimes were most egregious or most personal were marked. The rest just needed to die.

His next victim needed to be marked. Doc wasn't sure what it was about central Washington that attracted the most evil of the people he targeted, but the place seemed full of the most vile people Doc could imagine.

The next target would be his crown jewel. So far, at least. Doc had big plans. Plans that would put him on the same pedestal as John Wilkes Booth and Lee Harvey Oswald.

For now, though, the death of this next target would be the greatest stroke of vengeance he'd taken since he'd started his crusade.

Vengeance. He liked that word. Punishment inflicted or retribution exacted for an injury or wrong.

Punishment and retribution. Another word for that was justice. That was his mission. Justice.

He liked the word vengeance better. Justice was impartial. Vengeance was personal. Vengeance was meaningful.

People could evade justice. Vengeance would hunt them down.

“Every last one,” he whispered. “Every last one of them.”

# CHAPTER THIRTEEN

Horizon Intelligence looked like a business that had gone bankrupt. The parking lot was full of dust and debris, and the shrubs that lined the sidewalks were overgrown and haphazard. The building was dirty as well, the windows filmy and the concrete covered in cobwebs and droppings.

The interior was no better. A dejected receptionist sat behind a desk covered in stacks of paperwork. Stains covered the tile floor, and the decorative fountain in the middle of the lobby was bone dry.

The receptionist didn't even bother to greet the agents as they walked up. It wasn't until Faith spoke that the young woman even acknowledged their presence. "Good afternoon. I'm Special Agent Faith Bold. This is my partner, Special Agent Michael Prince, and my K9 unit, Turk. We need to speak with Guthrie Henderson."

The receptionist didn't seem at all surprised that FBI agents were here to see the CEO. Faith wondered how many other government agencies had arrived to interview him over the past year. "I'll let him know you're on your way up. He's the only office on the fifth floor."

"His office is the entire fifth floor?" Michael asked.

"Yep," the receptionist replied in an exceptionally bored tone. She dialed the number and when she hung up, she said, "Go ahead. He's waiting for you."

Faith and Michael exchanged a look with each other and headed for the elevator. The receptionist called after them, "The elevator doesn't work. You'll have to take the stairs."

They looked at each other again and headed for the stairs. Turk snorted, and Faith said, "I couldn't agree more."

As promised, Guthrie Henderson waited for them in his office, which, as also promised, did indeed take up the entire fifth floor. Faith stared incredulously at the opulent room, which sported three fish tanks, a massive tv screen, a full kitchen and a desk that stretched a full fifteen feet.

Guthrie himself was as drab as his office was garish. He was a short balding man who looked strikingly like a ten-years-older version of

Peter Olivera. He looked up at the agents and said, “All right. What is it this time?”

“Done this before, huh?” Michael asked.

“SEC, FTC, FBI, ATF, and about a dozen Senate and Congressional investigatory arms. You have a blow-by-blow account of every shit I’ve taken in the past ten years, so what could you possibly want from me now?”

“We’d like to know if you’re a serial killer,” Faith said.

Guthrie’s eyes snapped up to her. “What?”

“We’re here investigating the murders of Geoff Murray, Barrett Jones, and Gabriel Duke.”

“Gabe’s dead?”

“As a doornail,” Michael said, “and we think you might have had something to do with it.”

“You’re kidding me.”

“We don’t kid.”

Guthrie stared between the two of them. Then he chuckled, an anxious and bitter laugh. "Jesus. It just keeps getting better. All right. Let's talk then. Can we talk here, or is this a 'you have the right to remain silent' thing?"

“At the moment, no,” Faith replied. “We can start the conversation here, and if we feel there’s a reason to continue it somewhere else, we’ll make that call later.”

“Works for me,” Guthrie said, “sit anywhere you like.”

“We’ll stand for now,” Faith said. “Do you mind if Turk takes a look around your office?”

“Suit yourself. You might find a gram or two of weed somewhere. I went through a phase right after Gabe threw me under the bus. Hated the stuff. Just made me more anxious.”

“We’re not here about drugs,” Faith assured him, “what we need to know is what happened between you and Gabe.”

“Well,” Guthrie replied, “I hired him to represent my firm in Washington.”

“What is it your firm does again?”

He chuckled. “Well, now we scramble to convince the FTC, SEC, FBI and a few dozen other watchdog agencies that we’re not hiding assets somewhere. We’re just good ol’ broke boys and girls now.”

Faith sighed and rubbed her forehead. “Mr. Henderson, I’m certain that your personal tragedies are the most impactful thing in your life right now, but for the duration of this conversation, can we keep our answers focused on the murders?"

"Sure," Guthrie said. "My firm *used* to manufacture sensors and cameras for military and intelligence applications. We specialized in stealth designs that could be adapted to fit multiple platforms. The idea was to streamline data-gathering products and give the U.S. government a one-size-fits-all option for situational awareness in combat or high-risk, non-combat situations. Well, a few one-size-fits-most options, but you get the idea."

"And what happened after you hired Gabe to represent you?"

"He promised us that he would get us contracts. He said, and I quote the lying asshole verbatim, 'Spend whatever you need to ramp up production. You'll have buyers before you finish your first batch.' Well, fool that I am, I trusted him. Next thing I know, I get a form letter from his fucking secretary telling me that he's elected to discontinue our business relationship and pursue other options. He couldn't even tell me that himself. Fucking coward."

Guthrie's anxiety morphed into a look of rage, and his hands curled into fists.

"That must have pissed you off," Michael prompted.

"You think? I poured everything into this. And not just me, either. I know the office is fucking stupid. I realize that now. I definitely had a case of the me-me syndrome, but it's not just me he affected. I had to lay off one hundred eleven people. Do you know what it's like to have a hundred people asking me how they're supposed to feed their families?"

"I imagine it's very upsetting."

"Damn right." He shook his head. "I sued him for breach of contract, of course, but that went nowhere. The government didn't like me holding Gabe accountable to his promises. It seems that the 'other opportunities' he pursued were with one of the big names in the defense industry. They're powerful people, and as I'm sure you know, they don't play by the same rules everyone else does."

"That's infuriating," Faith said, "I would be really angry if someone did that to me. Maybe angry enough to kill them."

"Oh, I was." Faith lifted her eyebrow and Guthrie continued, "Yeah, I'm not going to lie. If you gave me a gun, a shot at Gabe, and ten seconds of immunity from prosecution, I'd empty the clip into his balls and let him bleed to death. The only reason I didn't is because it's been made very clear to me that I'm not one of those powerful people. The rules apply to me."

"That's a solid argument," Michael said, "but it's not quite a convincing one. Can you provide an alibi for your whereabouts two nights ago?"

"I've been sleeping here," he said, "but the security cameras don't work anymore, so I can't prove that. If you ask Shelly, she might confirm that I never left. Then again, she might not. She's still a kid. She doesn't care one way or another what happens to anything that isn't within eyesight."

"Shelly's the receptionist?"

"That's her. Real joy to be around, isn't she?"

"So here's the problem with that," Faith said, "Gabriel Duke was murdered very early in the morning. You would have had time to drive from here, kill him, and drive back before anyone could have noticed you."

Guthrie sighed. He lifted his hands and let them drop. "Well, I'm not sure how to help myself with that situation. I can tell you the truth and hope that you guys believe it, but…" he flipped his hands again.

"What about four nights ago?" Faith asked. "Gunnery Sergeant Barrett Jones, USMC. He was also murdered by the same killer. He was just on his way home to his family after meeting his unit at the Happy House."

"The Happy House? What is that, a strip club?"

"It's a bar in Pembroke off of the forty-two."

"Huh. Weird name for a bar."

"That's beside the point. Do you know anything about Barrett Jones?"

"Not beyond what you just told me. And my alibi is that I was here, where I've been every waking moment for the past three weeks and where I'll be until the last little shred of hope in my body finally dies and I accept a life renting rooms and taking the bus to my job as a cashier."

"Three weeks?" Faith asked.

"Yep. That's when we declared bankruptcy. I've stayed here making sure that all of the associated bullshit is taken care of."

"Like hiding assets?" Michael suggested.

"Feel free to look," Guthrie retorted. "Mi casa es su casa. In fact, feel free to take whatever you want. Might fetch a few bucks online if you find a weirdo who likes broken cameras."

Faith cast an irritated glance at Michael and brought the focus back to the case. "Do you have an alibi for November twelfth of last year?"

Guthrie stared at her a moment. Then he laughed. "November twelfth? Huh. That's funny."

"Why's that funny?"

"I actually *do* have an alibi for that. Wouldn't you know it. Maybe my luck hasn't entirely run out. Boy, I'll tell you, ninety-nine people out of a hundred would have no idea what they were doing on November twelfth of last year, but I do because I was at a defense conference in Chicago. The Defense Experimental Logistics and Intelligence Convention. Or the DELI convention because hey, acronyms, right?"

He tapped some keys on his phone, then turned it to show the agents. "Here. That's me."

Faith and Michael looked at the screen. It was an image of several men and women in expensive suits standing in front of a large mural with the DELI convention logo. Guthrie Henderson was in the front row, third from left.

"They put me in the front because I'm short. They were very clear about that. Not that I was important, just short. Guess that should have been my first clue that I was playing above my head."

Michael double-checked the website and verified that it was accurate. His disappointment showed on his face, and Guthrie said, "Sorry to let you down. If you need me to be a murderer, I can go kill myself if you want."

Faith frowned at the inappropriate joke. It wasn't her job to be anyone's moral compass, but sometimes she really wished it was. "I'm sorry for what happened to your business, Mr. Henderson," she said stiffly. "Thank you for your time."

"Of course. It was fun. Feel free to visit whenever you want. At least until they take the building from me too."

Turk trotted up, looking just as disappointed as Michael and Faith. He cast an irritated glance at Guthrie, who remarked, "Even the dog wishes I was guilty. Good times."

# CHAPTER FOURTEEN

They spent the first few minutes of the drive home in silence. Turk fell asleep, and Faith envied his ability to find rest at the drop of a hat. She herself had possessed that talent prior to her encounter with Trammell. Most combat veterans had the ability to sleep instantly and wake instantly, a skill that was critical in a job where action could happen at any moment and sleep was as precious as diamonds.

Trammell's attack on Faith had taken that from her. The psychological trauma she'd endured had healed in most ways, but she hadn't been able to recapture her ability to sleep whenever she needed.

Not that she needed sleep now. Her mind was too restless for sleep, even if she could have found it.

This case was like an endless series of false leads. Every thread they pulled came apart in their hands. None of those threads seemed to affect at all the Gordian knot that this case was.

She closed her eyes and tried to puzzle it out in her mind, but it remained out of reach, floating in her psyche but never coalescing into a recognizable answer. It was like building a ship out of bits of driftwood.

She wasn't getting anywhere with this.

*She opened her eyes and tried to sit back up but found she couldn't move. She frowned and pulled again, but her hands and legs were firmly bound to the chair. She turned to Michael to ask what was wrong, but Michael wasn't there.*

*She wasn't in the car. She was back in the barn—Trammell's barn. She was tied to the chair, and the only light came through a small crack high on the wall in front of her.*

*She tested her bonds, but as usual, they held firm. Her heart began to pound, and she reminded herself that this was only a dream. None of it was real. She just had to get through this, and then she would wake up and everything would be okay.*

*But the last dream had hurt. She wasn't sure how, but it had hurt. If her nightmares were going to come with a visceral reminder of the pain that Trammell had caused her, then it would be nearly impossible for her to survive them.*

*A sliver of light appeared in front of her, and a moment later, Trammell entered, his massive frame a forbidding shadow in the dim light.*

*"Well, well, well," he said, his high-pitched, lilting voice incongruous on a frame powerful enough to carry a five-hundred-pound donkey on his shoulders for miles. "If it isn't out little FBI agent come to visit."*

*Faith wondered why she always focused on his voice. What was it about that soft tenor that she always fixated on?*

*A voice answered her, this voice belonging to Franklin West, the Copycat Donkey Killer who had surpassed his inspiration, both for Faith and the world at large.*

*"You seek order, as all sheep do. So your mind fixates on anything disorderly and refuses to look away. It's so easy to distract you, Faith."*

*West walked from behind Faith to join Trammell in front of her. The two of them grinned malevolently at her, and Faith tested to see if she could speak. Sometimes her mouth was taped shut in these dreams, but tonight, she could talk.*

*"You told me the last time we spoke that I needed to see things from the perspective of my killers. What is my killer's perspective?"*

*West laughed. "Always the direct approach, Faith. Surely you don't expect your subconscious to hand you the answers to your problems in a bulleted list."*

*"Doesn't psychology teach that the subconscious can recognize things before the conscious mind can?"*

*"Bullshit psychology, yes. There's very little fact to back it up. But you didn't come here to argue with me."*

*"I didn't come here at all," Faith said. "If I could, I would never come here again."*

*"You did," West said. "Remember? For a long time, you were free of these nightmares. So why did you come back?"*

*Faith shook her head. "I didn't come here by choice." Trammell selected a knife from the tray, and Faith saw that tonight, the knife he held was a polished scalpel and not the rusty knife he typically used on her. "Believe me," she said as Trammell approached, a crazed gleam in his eye, "I would never revisit this if that was possible."*

*West sighed and shook his head. "You've said this to others before, Faith. There's always a choice."*

*Trammell slid the scalpel behind Faith's knee and sliced. A brilliant bolt of pain sliced through her leg, and she cried out, tears forming in her eyes. "I did not choose this!"*

*"You did. And so did your killer. Why?"*

*Trammell sliced the top of Faith's knee, and she shrieked. "I don't know! I don't fucking know!"*

*"I think you do, Faith. I think you know exactly why. I think you don't want to admit it, but I think you know."*

*Trammell sliced the underside of Faith's opposite knee, and Faith sobbed. "Tell me!"*

*"I can't," West said, "you won't let me."*

*Faith opened her eyes and stared at him through her tears. "What? I just told you to tell me!"*

*"So you did," West replied, "but you won't let me answer. I wonder why that is?"*

*Trammell sliced the top of her knee and Faith growled. "Well, fuck! I'll let you! Tell me!"*

*"You're trapped here, Faith. Michael's told you, I've told you, you've told yourself. Even David's told you. You never left this room. Not entirely. A piece of you has remained here and will until it decides to leave it behind."*

*Trammell severed Faith's Achilles tendon on her left side, and she cried out as a fresh wave of pain coursed through her.*

*"Your killer is trapped too, Faith. By his own volition. Or her, I suppose, though I rather think he's male. This sort of physical violence is rarely committed by a female."*

*Trammell severed the other Achilles' tendon, and Faith shuddered as a wave of nausea followed the pain. She would pass out soon, or, in this case, she would wake.*

*"We'll say he for the sake of argument," West said. "He's trapped. Not here, obviously, but somewhere. Wherever he's trapped is leading him to murder his victims, not that he sees it that way."*

*"He's trapped somewhere and being trapped is leading him?" Faith asked. "That makes no sense."*

*Trammell flicked the scalpel across Faith's cheek, splitting the skin and sending rivulets of blood down her cheek.*

*"Sense," West said. "Order. Logic. Right and wrong."*

*Each word brought a fresh stroke with the scalpel. Faith felt her vision swimming as the blood loss overcame her.*

*"You are obsessed with this, Faith," West said, leaning down until his eyes met hers. "You are obsessed with this, and so, you cannot look away." He stood and backed off, and Tramell's looming figure replaced his. "And so, you cannot leave."*

*Trammell leaned down. Faith could smell his sour breath as it passed his rotting, yellowed teeth. He grabbed a fistful of her hair and yanked her head back, then pressed the scalpel to her throat. "Let's see how you bleed, little girl."*

*He sliced her throat open.*

***

Faith gasped and sat bolt upright in the chair.

"Jesus!" Matt cried out.

The vehicle swerved right, then left, as Michael narrowly avoided driving off the road. His eyes snapped to Faith. "What happened? What's wrong?"

Turk was instantly awake. He stood in between them and looked at Faith with concern.

"I'm all right," she said. "I had another nightmare. I'm fine."

"Are you sure?" Matt asked.

Faith took a deep breath and reminded herself that Matt was only trying to be helpful. "Yes," she said, "I'm sure."

"All right," Matt said. "Well, we'll be back in Pembroke in a few minutes, so try to avoid napping, okay?"

She glared at him. "Was that supposed to be funny?"

"Not at all," he said, "I just want to go home to Ellie when this is over and rolling a police cruiser off the road in the ass-end of middle-of-nowhere, Washington seems like a bad way to make that happen."

"So learn how to drive," she quipped.

Turk started licking her face, and she laughed and pushed him away. "I'm fine. Really, I am."

Turk didn't seem convinced, and neither did Michael.

"You okay?"

"I'm fine," she replied. Then, to change the subject before he pressed her, she asked, "So things are better between you and Ellie then?"

"They're good enough," he replied.

She lifted an eyebrow. "That bad, huh?"

He frowned at her. "Since when are you so interested in my relationship?"

"You're my friend," she said, "I want to make sure that you're okay."

"I'm okay." He sighed. "Look, it's… Ellie just isn't going to be happy as long as my job involves putting my life in danger. I've come home with bruises from the last few cases, and she doesn't want her husband to end up dying forty years before his time."

"Is that all it is?" Faith asked.

"Yes. Why do you ask?"

Faith didn't reply. In the past, Michael and Ellie had argued over Michael's continued professional partnership with Faith. The two of them had once been lovers, though only briefly and not for years. Still, Michael spent more time with Faith than he did with Ellie since they worked closely together, and Ellie was understandably jealous. Faith hoped that her growing relationship with David would soften some of the tension, but it occurred to her now that Ellie's trouble with her was based on more than just her past relationship with Michael. From Ellie's perspective, Faith was deeply troubled. She had twice suspected Ellie of being the Copycat Killer, and their encounters had been… less than cordial.

"It isn't because of you," Michael said shortly, guessing the reason for Faith's silence. "She's not jealous."

"I didn't say anything," Faith said.

"You didn't have to."

Faith sighed. "I didn't mean to hurt your feelings, Michael. I'm sorry."

They rode in silence for another few minutes. Michael broke it when he said, "I'm sorry, Faith. I…" he sighed. "Things with Ellie have actually been pretty rough. She's pushing for me to commit to retiring."

Faith looked at him. "*Commit* to retiring? You mean you're considering it?"

"Well, yeah. I've been considering it. You and I talked about it."

"We talked about it, but I didn't know that you were giving it serious thought."

"I *told* you I was," Michael said irritably. "I don't want to end up like the Boss. Much respect to the man, but the only reason he hasn't drunk himself to death is because he has godlike willpower. My willpower is not godlike, and I spend a few too many minutes staring wistfully at the single malts when I go shopping these days." He sighed. "I'm not like you, Faith. I believe that you can do this for the rest of your life. I believe that they'll have to drag you kicking and screaming into retirement. Me?" He tightened his grip on the steering wheel as though steeling himself for an argument. "There are more important things to me than this job."

Faith actually had considered retirement as recently as the night they had started this case. Staring down at David's broken body had made her realize that there was a limit to what she could endure. Leaving was out of the question as long as West was at large, but after…

"I understand," she said quietly.

Michael looked at her with surprise. His grip relaxed, and he nodded and said, "Well, whatever happens, I'll keep you up to date. And don't worry. I'm not going to move across the country and change my number and stop talking to you."

"Doesn't Ellie want you to move across the country?"

"Let's not talk about Ellie anymore," Matt demurred. "Besides, we're back in Pembroke. We need to figure out our next move."

"Can we figure it out over lunch?" Faith asked. "I'm starving."

Michael grinned and pulled into the parking lot of a diner. "I thought you'd never ask.

## CHAPTER FIFTEEN

Michael bit into the largest hamburger Faith had ever seen and sighed contentedly. "Oh yeah," he said, "that hits the spot."

Faith took a bit of her own, much more reasonably sized, burger and felt a similar rush of satisfaction. "Wow. This is *really* good."

Turk happily chowed down on his strip steak, his face lit up with contentment. She smiled down at him and thought again of how nice it would be if he could spend the last few years of his life like a dog and not chasing down violent criminals.

"See," Michael said, "this is what beef should taste like. None of that grass-fed, organic, soy-based bullshit."

Faith smiled. "I don't think you can have grass-fed soybeans."

"Whatever. You get my point. Good food isn't supposed to be healthy."

"I don't think you're entirely aware of what you're saying," she said, "but I'm grateful for this hamburger anyway."

"You know," Michael said, taking another bite.

"I'm sure you'll tell me in a few minutes when you're done chewing," Faith teased.

Michael lifted his middle finger, and she laughed. He swallowed and said, "I was going to say that you can be really annoying when you get pedantic like that."

"Well, get used to it," she said, "because I have no plans to change anytime soon."

"Thanks for the warning."

She took a bite of her own burger and thought back to her dream. West—or the image her subconscious had created of him—said that the killer was trapped. But where? When? Why?

"How and wherefore?" she muttered.

"What's that?"

She sighed. "In my dream, I…" she thought about it and decided it would be a waste of time to try to explain the conversations she'd been having with herself. "Well, it doesn't matter. The point is that I think our killer is stuck somewhere in the past."

"Where?"

"That's the question. It would have to be somewhere and something that gives him a reason to hate these victims. In fact, he might not see it as hate. He might see it as protection."

"Like he's protecting his victims? Is that what the cuts are? Some sort of ritual?"

"No," she said. "The word vengeance makes it clear that he sees this as a punishment. But I think he also sees it as protection."

"From what?"

She thought a moment. "From war," she finally said. "All of our victims were involved in war one way or another. Geoff Murray sold weapons, Gabriel Duke lobbied for a greater defense budget. Barrett Jones was a sniper."

"It seems a little unfair to group Jones with the others, though," Michael said. "That's like shooting a tiger and a bear, then tracking down a single wasp. I know that's a shitty metaphor, but do you see what I mean?"

"Yes," she said. "Jones was a much smaller fish compared to the others."

"So why him? I could see someone being on a mission to kill people like Murray and Duke, but Jones just makes no sense."

"I agree," Faith said, "and that makes him the key."

"The part that makes no sense is the key?"

"Making that part make sense is the key," she explained, "or rather, figuring out why that part makes sense."

"So why does killing Jones make sense?"

Faith sighed and leaned back in her chair. "Why would the killer feel trapped in the same place as Jones? Or maybe he felt trapped because of Jones?" She shook her head. "I feel like we're circling the answer, but we can't quite reach it."

"I feel like we find a different answer every ten minutes and then just as quickly find out why that answer is bullshit."

"Yeah," Faith said.

She set her burger down and steepled her fingers. "What the hell are we missing?" she asked softly.

Her phone rang, and she and Michael exchanged a look. They knew what this phone call was.

With a sinking feeling, she answered. "Bold."

She listened to the Pembroke PD dispatch officer, and her heart completed its journey to the floor. "Understood. We're on our way."

She hung up and smiled dejectedly at Matt. "Well, we have some fresh evidence to look at."

He sighed and dropped his burger. "Goddammit."

"Yeah," she agreed. "My thoughts exactly."

***

Faith and Michael stared somberly at the body in front of them. This woman had been killed the same way as the other victims and staged the same way as well. Like the first two, she had been killed elsewhere—a field of tall grass a hundred yards off the road—and moved to the place where she had been found, in this case a call box. She had been propped up to a sitting position and remained there, her head slumped forward on her chest.

*She* happened to be Congresswoman Belinda Montclair of Tennessee's Seventh Congressional District. She happened to be a very active proponent of increased military spending and what pundits described as the "bomb first, count bodies later," movement.

Her death was easily the most high-profile of their victims so far, and probably the most high-profile of their career.

"This is going to be an issue when the press finds out about it," Michael said.

"This is an issue now," Faith replied.

"Yeah, but it's going to be a bigger issue when we have microphones in our faces everywhere we go."

"Yeah," Faith agreed. "Dammit."

"We should call the Boss," Michael said. "He's going to want to be aware of the blowback from this."

Faith sighed. "Yes, but let's wait until we look at the scene. When we call, I want to be able to give him concrete evidence that we're on top of things. The last thing either of us need is a dressing-down."

"Good point."

The three of them got to work examining the scene. Turk trotted into the field, nose to the ground, looking for evidence along the path of the murder. Michael looked around the call box, trying to find footprints or tire marks or any other kind of physical evidence that could be useful.

Faith looked at the body. She squatted down and stared at Montclair's body, trying to imagine what the killer saw.

Montclair was one of the younger members of Congress. At thirty-nine years old, she wasn't overly youthful in appearance, but she was a strikingly attractive woman, a fact she used to great effect to advance her career and her positions in Congress. Faith put gloves on and carefully lifted her head. Montclair's sliced throat looked horrific, but Faith ignored that for the moment and tried to think what she would have looked like alive.

She had almost flawless features, symmetrical and just angular enough to make her appear strong without also looking severe. Her eyes were dull and filmy now, but in life, they would have been a brilliant green.

She was beautiful, but beauty wasn't a motive for this killer. Gabriel Duke was as attractive as Montclair, but Barrett Jones was average-looking, and Geoff Murray was, in Faith's opinion, a few ticks closer to ugly than average.

So what else was she?

She was influential. Her beauty was just a tool at the end of the day. She, like all of their victims, had the ability to impact the waging of wars. Like Duke, she had the ability to influence defense policy.

Like Barrett…

She wasn't like Barrett. That was the frustrating part. That was the missing link. An arms dealer, a defense lobbyist, and a very pro-military congresswoman. That all made sense.

So why Jones? Why a former Marine who just wanted to drink with his buddies every now and then and hang out with his family during the day?

She sighed and studied the wounds. They were as precise and careful as before. The single stab wound to the heart that killed Montclair, and the cuts to the arms and throat that matched the other victims. The word vengeance was written in front of her this time rather than above her due to the call box's small size, but other than the location, everything was exactly the same.

Vengeance for what?

West's words from her dream came back to her. *"Your mind fixates on anything disorderly and refuses to look away. It's so easy to distract you, Faith."*

Barret was disorderly. The word vengeance was disorderly, or at least an order she didn't understand.

So what was consistent? What was ordered?

The method was ordered. It was, in a macabre way, elegant, even artistic.

Was this killer using art to send a message? Well, he was, clearly, but was it intentional? Was that the point?

That could explain Barrett. He might prefer high-profile victims, but maybe the urge had struck him before he was aware of high-profile victims. It might have been enough for him to have a symbol of war he could deface.

And what was the message? That war bled nations dry? Or was it more personal, that war bled people dry? And how would the killer's actions be informed by that personal connection?

She hated coming back to the personal connection after it had failed them several times already, but her mind kept returning. She heard West's mocking voice in her mind and pushed it away. She had found killers this way before. If nothing else was coming to mind now, then she should at least pursue the one lead she actually had.

She felt for Montclair's cell phone, and when she found it, she pulled it from Montclair's pocket. It had been a long time since Faith had taken the cybercrimes course at the Academy, and a lot had changed since then.

Well, if she couldn't get into the cell phone here, she could have Pembroke PD look at it. Assuming Pembroke had a cybercrimes division. If they didn't, she would have to send it to the Seattle Field Office, and if she did that, it would be days before they were able to learn anything from it.

She had to get in now.

She opened the phone and attached a small usb flash drive she carried at all times on duty but had never used until now to the charging port. The screen flickered and then rebooted. When it rebooted, it opened to Montclair's home screen, bypassing the password screen.

Faith pumped her fist in victory and began looking through Montclair's texts. She felt a touch uneasy going through the private communications of a dead woman, but if she could get any evidence at all, she was sure Montclair's spirit would forgive her for the violation.

The texts from her family were hard to read. She had a husband and three children ranging from eleven to fifteen. It broke Faith's heart to see the loving texts from all of them.

"I'm so sorry, guys," she said softly. "I'm so sorry."

She opened another text thread, labeled, CLEANERS, and her heart didn't feel so broken anymore. Unless Faith was greatly mistaken, most people didn't send nude photos of themselves to their cleaners, and most cleaners didn't talk at length about how appealing they found particular parts of their employers' bodies.

So Mrs. Montclair was having an affair.

Faith pulled out her own phone and logged into the FBI database. A few keystrokes brought her to the phone number search, and she plugged in Mr. CLEANERS' number.

The match came up to Aaron Blakely.

Mr. Blakely was an artist, a sculptor, to be exact. He lived in Miller, Washington and was known for his disturbingly violent creations, many of which featured realistic wounds, death masks and copious amounts of blood-colored paint and stains.

One image in particular caught Faith's eye. It was of a woman on a cross with her arms outstretched. Her throat and arms were cut, and above her was a capstone with the label MARTYR.

The name of the piece was VENGEANCE SATISFIED.

She called for Michael and showed him the image. His eyes widened. "Huh. Nice piece."

"Isn't it?" Faith agreed, "I think it's very informative, don't you?"

"Well, I've always believed that if you truly want to understand the meaning of a work of art, you should talk to the artist."

"That's an excellent idea," Faith said. "Let's go see what Mr. Blakely has to say."

# CHAPTER SIXTEEN

"I take it Mr. Blakely's art isn't paying the bills as well as he would have hoped," Michael said.

Faith looked out her window at the dilapidated houses and unkempt yards of the neighborhood through which they drove and had to agree. This was the kind of place people lived when they hit rock bottom.

Occasionally, they would pass a house with a huge guard dog that barked aggressively at Turk. Turk kept a professional demeanor as he always did, but his eyes narrowed a little. In past cases, he had been forced to fight against dangerous dogs. He'd come out on top each time, but there had been some near misses.

Faith reached over to stroke his fur. He started a little, then relaxed under her attention. She smiled at him, but her smile faded when Michael pulled to a stop in front of Blakely's address.

Blakely's house wasn't in worse shape than the other houses, but it was easily the most forbidding. That wasn't really the house's fault, though. Faith just couldn't imagine many people would find the dozens of horrifying statues that crowded his front yard very inviting.

"Seems like a well-adjusted individual," Michael quipped.

Faith shook her head and offered no comment.

The three agents left the car and started toward the house. The gate was locked, but when Faith tested the lock, it came apart in their hands. Normally, it would be a breach of protocol to enter someone else's property without permission or a warrant, but the statues in the yard and the connection he had to their most recent victim gave them plenty of probable cause.

They started up the yard, passing sculptures of frightened and anguished people in the throes of death set among the vacant faces of those who had already died. As they neared the front door, Faith saw the statue that reminded her of their crime scene.

When Michael saw it, he muttered, "Jesus."

"Looks like his best piece," Faith commented. "I'd really love to know what his creative process was here."

"Yeah," Michael said, "I can't say I feel the same way, but I guess I don't have a choice."

Turk growled low in his throat, and Faith reached down to pat his shoulder. "Easy boy," she said, "we'll be all right."

She knocked on the door, but as soon as her fist connected, it swung wide open. The three agents paused, listening intently for any sound or sign of movement. When they didn't hear anything after several seconds, Faith drew her weapon and looked at Michael.

He sighed and drew his own weapon. "Semper fi."

"Don't say that."

"What? Why?"

"You're not a Marine."

"Really?"

"Really."

He stared at her a moment, then shrugged and said, "Okay. How about let's get the bastard?"

"That works."

"Then let's get the bastard."

They walked inside, and the moment they stepped inside, Faith's sense of unease grew.

Blakely was more well-known as a sculptor, but he didn't limit himself to that medium. His walls were covered with portraits—some hand-drawn, some painted and some photographed—of various naked women. Apparently, he got around.

One of the women was Montclair. Another was Lindsey Murray, who, it seemed, was not so devoted to her husband as she seemed. Another was Susanne Duke. It looked like Blakely had motive for nearly all of their victims.

Faith felt mixed emotions when none of the photographs turned out to be of Leah Jones. She was relieved to know that Leah wasn't among the unfortunately large number of military spouses who were cheating on their significant others, but if she had been, it would have connected Barrett to the other victims and given Blakely a reason to want him dead.

As it was, he was still the outlier. Maybe Blakely could shed some light on that when they found him.

"Hey," Michael called from the other end of the room. "Check this out."

Faith walked to him and chuckled humorlessly when she saw what he was pointing out. "Can't say I'm surprised."

"What kind of person frames it, though? That's some next-level weirdness."

“It” happened to be a court order from the State of Washington instructing Mr. Aaron Blakely to inform his neighbors of his status as a registered sex offender, a fact he was also ordered to display by placing the provided notice on a sign in his front yard.

Well, he hadn’t posted the sign, but Faith thought his choice of lawn ornaments warning enough.

Turk growled low in his throat. She followed his eyes to the hallway and found Aaron Blakely staring at them in shock, a duffle bag in one hand.

He was an attractive enough man, she supposed, if you liked bad boys. He had a goatee and close-cropped spiked hair, which was a heavily salted light brown. He was in great shape, trim and well-muscled, which made sense considering his occupation. What really captured Faith's attention though were his deep-set gray eyes and stout jaw. He looked mean. Faith wasn't one to judge someone on appearance alone, but there were quite a few other indicators that suggested Aaron’s appearance was an accurate representation of his personality.

“Aaron Blakely?” Faith said. “I’m Special Agent—”

She didn’t get a chance to finish. With a grunt, Blakely heaved the duffel bag at Faith. She sidestepped, avoiding the impact, but Michael wasn’t so lucky. He caught the duffel bag, but its weight caused him to stagger backwards, allowing Blakely to pass them, narrowly avoiding Turk’s snapping jaws.

They gave chase, but Blakely reached the yard before they could reach him and began throwing his sculptures down to impede their way. Turk navigated the sculptures faster than the human agents did and caught up to Blakely just past his front gate.

Blakely squealed in a decidedly unmanly voice when Turk's jaws snapped shut around his ankle. Turk had caught only the pants, however, and with a mighty tug, Blakely ripped his leg free. He ran toward his car, but by this time, Michael and Faith had reached the gate.

Michael reached Blakely first, grabbing him and keeping him from getting into his car, an old Saturn Ion sedan which also clashed with his bad boy persona.

*Fits with the starving artist part*, Faith thought.

Michael outweighed Blakely by a good twenty-five pounds, but he still struggled to hold him. Blakely finally gave up on the car when he saw Turk bearing down on him. He grabbed Michael’s wrist and dropped his weight, tossing Michael over his shoulder.

Turk leapt at him, and he ducked under the dog, then drove his fist straight into Faith's midsection. Her wind fled, and she collapsed to the ground, gasping for air.

Blakely took off down the street, moving with impressive speed. Turk looked at Faith with concern, but she waved for him to chase Blakely. He turned toward the fleeing criminal and bared his teeth, then sprinted after him.

Michael helped Faith to her feet, and they watched as Turk easily caught the fleeing man. He leapt in the air and planted all four paws on Blakely's back, shoving him to the ground. Blakely rolled over and slammed his fist into the side of Turk's head, staggering the dog and sending him stumbling away.

"Turk!" Faith shouted as her wind came back. "Blakely, I swear to God, if you hurt my dog again, I'll shoot you!"

Blakely looked at Faith, who was now sprinting towards him and decided she was serious. He got to his feet and continued to run. Faith dropped to Turk's side. "Hey boy," she said. "Look at me. Are you all right?"

Turk shook his head, his legs shaking as he struggled to regain his composure. Michael continued onward, running Blakely down again—pretty impressive considering the difference in athleticism.

Blakely spun, driving his fist toward Michael's midsection, but Michael was ready for it. He parried the blow and sent his own left hook into Blakely's temple. The blow lifted Blakely completely off the ground, and he fell heavily onto his side.

Amazingly, though, he popped right back to his feet and started sending a flurry of blows Michael's way. Michael might have had the power advantage, but Blakely had the speed advantage, and several of the blows found their mark. Finally, one hard overhand hit Michael's temple, and he fell to his knees.

Blakely drew his leg back to kick at Michael but thought better of it when he saw Faith and Turk bearing down on him. He turned to run, but Michael grabbed his ankle and pulled hard. Blakely tripped and nearly fell. When Faith tackled him, he fell all of the way.

He rolled onto his back and lifted his hand to strike Faith, but Turk stopped next to him, teeth bared, eyes blazing, and barked a warning at him. Blakely paled, and Faith said, "I'd stay still if I were you. He doesn't like seeing me get hurt."

Blakely gulped and opened his fist. "Good boy," Faith said.

She rolled him over and handcuffed him, then pulled him to his feet. “All right, tough guy,” she said, “let’s go somewhere nice and quiet and have a cordial conversation.”

# CHAPTER SEVENTEEN

Blakely held his chin high and his eyelids half-shut in the classic street-tough pose. He lifted his chin in greeting when the agents entered. Faith rolled her eyes, and Michael chuckled.

Turk didn't seem to see the humor in it. He stared at Blakely coldly, and Faith wondered if Blakely would act so tough if he knew how much Turk wanted to hurt him.

The agents sat across from him, and Blakely grinned at Michael. "You've got a good left hand, man. Almost had me out."

"Thank you," Michael said drily. "Maybe I'll visit you in prison and give you some lessons."

"Yeah, I'm not going to prison," Blakely said. "I didn't do anything wrong."

"Let's see," Faith said, "resisting arrest, assault on a peace officer—aggravated assault, actually and multiple counts—and, oh yeah, how about four counts of murder?"

Blakely blinked. "Murder?"

"Yep. Geoff Murray, Barrett Jones, Gabriel Duke and Belinda Montclair."

"Okay, I recognize all of those names but Jones. Did I fuck his wife too?"

Faith concealed her disappointment at hearing Blakely deny knowledge of Jones. Dammit, was he just a one-off?

"Then you know that all four of them are dead."

"Well, yeah. You just told me."

"How did they die?"

"How would I know? I didn't kill anyone."

"So what are the sculptures about?" Michael asked.

"It's art," Blakely said haughtily. "I wouldn't expect you to understand."

"For your sake, I hope that's not true," Michael said, "because if you can't give me a better reason than 'I'm a murderer and like making things that look like murder,' I'm going to go with the thought that you're a murderer."

"That's not gonna hold up in court," Blakely said smugly.

"Well," Faith replied, "the naked pictures of three of our victims' wives along with a statue that looks an awful lot like the way our victims were staged after their murders is going to go a long way. Not to mention the texts between you and Montclair that we found and the texts that we will find when we subpoena Susanne Duke's and Lindsey Murray's phones."

Blakely's smile faded.

"Oh, now we're taking this seriously," Michael said. "Wonderful. So let's talk. Let's start with the easy one that we already know your answer to. Did you kill Geoff Murray, Barrett Jones, Gabriel Duke and Belinda Montclair?"

"No."

"Figured you'd say that. Next question: why were you sleeping with Lindsey Murray, Susanne Duke and Belinda Montclair?"

Blakely lifted his chin proudly. "What can I say? Every now and then a woman wants a real man in her bed." He grinned lasciviously at Faith. "You understand, right, sweetheart?"

Faith's lip curled in disgust, and Blakely chuckled. He looked at Michael and asked, "You ever hit that?"

"You? Yeah, I have. Want me to hit it again?"

Faith put an arm on Michael's shoulder to calm him, and Blakely chuckled again. "Yep. You hit it. Was it good? I'll bet it was good. Good girls are only good until you get their legs open, am I right?"

Faith leaned forward. "Blakely, I'm sure you feel quite proud of yourself for your sexual conquests, and hey, I'm sure those women enjoyed it too. Based on the texts I read, Belinda Montclair sure did. At least until she didn't. Tell me, how did you feel when she told you she didn't want to see you anymore? I'll help you out before you answer: I read all of the texts you sent her, so lying to me would only prove to me that you're as stupid as you look, and that would be a bad idea for you right now."

Blakely's smile disappeared again. "Yeah, I was upset. I sent some angry messages. I wasn't going to do anything about it, though."

"Angry messages," Faith repeated. "Hmm. Let's look at some of those angry messages."

She pulled Montclair's cell phone from her pocket, and Blakely paled a shade.

"Let's see," she said, "Ah, here's a good one." She cleared her throat and read, "'You don't get to leave, bitch. I'm done when I say I'm done. You belong to me, you slut whore.'"

Blakely chuckled, but this time there was far more anxiety than humor.

"Here's another. 'I will make you wish you had never been born. I'll cut you and watch you bleed, you stuck-up bitch.'"

"Like I said—" Blakely began.

"Ah ah," Faith said, holding up a finger. "Let me read you my favorite. 'I'll cut your veins and your throat at the same time and leave you where everyone can see what a worthless slut you are.'"

Blakely didn't finish the sentence he had started.

"Now," Faith said, "if I read the texts you sent the other women, will I see a similar pattern of threatening behavior?"

Blakely didn't answer.

"You have the right to remain silent," Faith said, "just know that we *will* be looking at those cell records. Emails and messaging apps, too. Social media, online chat rooms, postal service records—any way a person could possibly communicate with another person. We'll also be interrogating them to learn everything there is to know about you."

Blakely sighed. "Yeah, I wanted to scare them, but I didn't want to kill them. I just… I didn't like feeling like a toy."

Michael laughed. "That's funny."

"Yeah?" Blakely snapped. "Maybe I'll fuck your wife too. Maybe I'll cut you, you fat pig."

Michael smiled. "You have quite the temper, don't you, Mr. Blakely?"

Blakely realized his mistake and frowned. "Yeah, whatever. I never killed anyone."

"You just threaten to kill them."

"As a joke."

"And yet, they all end up dead. All within a half hour of where you live. All shortly after they or their wives conclude an affair with you."

"Well, I didn't kill them," Blakely insisted petulantly. "I don't know what to tell you."

"You can start by telling us where you were last night."

He sneered, "I was with Belinda. Inside her, above her, underneath her, all around her."

He realized his mistake again too late, and this time, his attitude vanished. "But I didn't kill her! She was alive when she left! I swear to God!"

"Lots of evil people swear to God," Faith said. "I imagine He's about as tired of it as we are."

“Look…” Blakely looked left and right between them. “Can’t you track her cell phone or something and prove that I didn’t kill her?”

“We can tell you where her cell phone is now,” Faith said, “not where it was last night.”

“Shit.” Blakely looked really nervous now.

“Here’s another point,” Faith said. “How is it that she ends up in your bed last night after you repeatedly threatened to kill her.”

“Look, I…” his voice trailed off. “I don’t want to tell you because I feel like you’re just going to think I’m being an asshole.”

“It’s way too late to convince me otherwise,” Faith said, “so focus on trying to convince me that you’re not a murderer.”

Blakely’s lower lip trembled. He looked so pathetic that Faith’s lip curled upward in disgust again. “Well, she… she had a humiliation kink.”

“A humiliation kink?”

“Yeah. She liked being called names and being forced to… do stuff. Not forced!” he quickly corrected. “Not really. Just… like roleplay.”

“I get the point,” Faith said. “So she came over because what, she enjoyed hearing you threaten to kill her?”

“No. She… look, I don’t know what to tell you. She wanted me, and I gave her what she wanted. That’s all.”

“What about two nights ago?” Faith asked. “Any alibi for that?”

“I was home.”

“Can you prove that?”

“Don’t you guys have to prove I wasn’t?”

“We do. I have a feeling it won’t be too hard to convince a judge considering what we have so far.”

“Gotta say,” Michael added. “It was decidedly uninspired to make a piece that almost exactly matches your murders.”

“I didn’t kill anyone!”

“What about four nights ago?” Faith asked. “Do you have an alibi for that?”

“Yes!” he said desperately. “I was at the Happy House. It’s a bar on—”

“We’re familiar,” Faith interrupted. “Care to guess why?”

Blakely looked between the two agents. “Wait. Was that? Was that Jones guy one of the Marines?”

“Fascinating,” Michael said. “I wonder how you happened to know that?”

“I just guessed.”

"Damned lucky guess."

"Man, I didn't kill him! I didn't kill anyone!"

"Here's the thing," Faith said, "We have proof that you threatened Belinda Montclair. We have you admitting to being in her company the night of her murder—after you threatened her. We have you admitting to being at the same place Barrett Jones was murdered. We have no alibi for you for either of the past three murders. We have substantial evidence that you had sexual relationships with one of our victims and the wives of two others. We have you celebrating your criminal past as a sex offender, and we have a sculpture of yours that is nearly an identical match to the wounds and—if you'll permit me—artwork at the scenes of all of our victims' murders. Can you see why we have a hard time believing you weren't involved in their deaths?"

Blakely was shaking from head to toe now. "Please," he whispered. "I didn't kill anyone. I was just having fun."

"Be that as it may," Faith said, "We're looking at a mountain of evidence pointing your way and not a lot of convincing reasons to ignore it."

Blakely took a shuddering breath to steady himself and said, "I'd like to have a lawyer present to continue this interview."

Faith and Michael looked at each other, then back at Blakely. "We'll get you a lawyer."

***

Faith and Michael watched as the officer led a very subdued Blakely to a cell. His lawyer wouldn't arrive until the following morning, effectively suspending continued interrogation until then.

"I love how the ones who act the toughest always crack the hardest under pressure," Michael said. "It never fails."

When Faith didn't respond right away, Michael looked at her. "You okay?"

She shook her head. "Jones still doesn't fit."

"What are you talking about? He was at the bar with Jones. Of course, he fits."

"He was there," Faith said, "but there's no motive. He was sleeping with Murray's and Duke's wives. He was sleeping with Montclair. He wasn't sleeping with Leah Jones. He didn't recognize Barrett's name."

"He *said* he doesn't recognize his name. That doesn't mean it's true."

"Yes, but he didn't really do a good job of hiding anything else. He clearly isn't the smartest tool in the shed. I don't see him hiding the fact that he knew Jones but admitting to knowing every other victim and bragging about sleeping with one of them hours before her death. It doesn't line up."

Michael sighed. "Not everything is going to fit in a neat little box, Faith. Sometimes things just don't make sense."

*You seek order, as all sheep do.*

"You're right," she said.

But…

"It just doesn't make sense. He thinks to hide Jones out of all of his victims?"

"Maybe Jones is the one he feels guilty about. He wasn't the husband of one of his flings. He wasn't a big shot in government or the arms world. He was a little guy, a Marine combat veteran. Even serial killers respect combat veterans. Maybe he genuinely feels bad about him, and even his own mind won't let him face the fact that he killed him."

"Maybe," Faith said, "but it doesn't make sense."

"Well," Michael said, "It'll make sense soon enough, or else his lawyer is going to help him find a way to convince us that it'll never make sense. I'm going to order some pizza. You want input on the toppings?"

She shook her head, and Michael laid a hand on her shoulder. "Hey. We worked hard for this. Don't deny yourself just because it seems too easy now that we've finally found the answer."

"It just doesn't seem right to me," she said. "I know that's not a scientific reason, but… it feels like we're missing something."

"I've learned better than to question your hunches," Michael said. "If you feel we need to look elsewhere, then I support you. But the evidence *does* point to Blakely. I think we pull both threads and see which one leads to our killer. We have enough to suspect Blakely, but not enough to convict him. If we follow that path a little further and find that there isn't enough to prove he's our killer, then we'll know."

"I'm just afraid we'll end up with another body while we're making sure."

"Well, I'm afraid that if we dismiss him, he'll give us another body."

She met his eyes, and he took his hand off of her shoulder. "Like I said, if you want to look elsewhere, I support you. But I don't think it's wise to dismiss Blakely on a feeling."

She nodded. "You're right. I just… God, I hate when things don't make sense."

*So your mind fixates on anything disorderly and refuses to look away.*

"Well, there's a good reason for that," she said.

"Good reason for what?" Michael asked.

She shook her head. "Nothing. Just thinking out loud."

"As long as you're thinking and not just going crazy on me."

"I've been crazy. You should be used to it by now."

"You know, you'd think I would be, but I keep expecting to go to work and find you well-adjusted."

"I can't help you with that."

He chuckled and said, "Well, as long as we're working late tonight, I'm going to get us some dinner."

He left, and she sat at the table in the break room and tried to piece together the puzzle in front of her.

The evidence all pointed to Blakely. Michael was right about that. The problem was that the evidence pointed to all of their suspects. That was why they were suspects in the first place. It wasn't enough.

*You seek order, Faith. As all sheep do.*

"There's a reason for that too."

Turk lifted his head from where it rested on his paws and looked up at her. She reached down and stroked his fur. "Nothing, boy. Mommy's just going crazy."

That was a common enough occurrence that Turk lowered his head and promptly went back to sleep. She smiled down at him and allowed her gratitude to soften her doubts.

But not remove them. She had work to do.

# CHAPTER EIGHTEEN

Corporal Candace Rogers, USMC, Candy to her boyfriend and Candy Girl to her brothers and sisters of Platoon C, Bravo Company, 4th Infantry Battalion—and *only* to them, left her house in good spirits.

As good as they could be anyway. Owl's death had cast a pall over everything. It was bad enough that Carter bit it last year, but losing Owl was in many ways an even harder blow to the remaining men and women of Platoon C. Owl was their rock, their pillar. He was the one everyone else went to when they were struggling, the one they could trust when they were afraid to go even to the others in the unit. It didn't make sense that he could be dead.

And at home, too. Dammit, they were supposed to be okay. How was it that they could survive the suck only to be taken by some crazy asshole back home? Was this what they were fighting for?

Obviously not. There were many millions more innocent people than guilty people. She didn't regret her choices despite the suffering it brought her. But damn, it sucked to lose people at home.

"The real suck is the suck you come home to," she said aloud.

She chuckled at that and decided it was a good thing she could still laugh. When you stopped laughing was when you needed to worry. Carter had stopped laughing.

Candace wouldn't stop laughing. She owed it to her family. She owed it to her boyfriend. She owed it to herself.

Most importantly, she owed it to her brothers and sisters. With Owl gone, they needed each other now more than ever.

So, although her heart was heavy, she kept her head high and pushed her spirits to follow. Today was the anniversary of the unit's first deployment together. She wore her ceremonial dress blues, freshly pressed, and wore her hair in the tight bun the Corps specified. Her shoes were polished to a high shine, and her medals gleamed where they hung from her jacket pocket.

She almost never wore her medals. Like many Marines, she thought it a little silly to celebrate people for doing their duty. The unit patch on her battle fatigues mattered far more to her than her Bronze Star did.

One medal, however, carried sentimental value. She looked down at the Purple Heart and thought of the day she had earned it. The Company was pinned down under heavy fire from insurgents. The Humvee Candace rode in with the rest of her squad had been destroyed by an IED, and all but three of the squad were dead.

She had dragged herself from the stricken vehicle and crawled behind the smoldering chassis of another Humvee and returned fire against the insurgents. They managed to hold out until the Air Force showed up and blasted the insurgents from the battlefield.

"Sanitized," was the word they used. She hated that word. Nothing about war was clean. It was dirty and violent and painful and frightening, and she longed for the day when people would find better things to do than kill each other.

But she had fought through it, and as her Purple Heart reminded her, she had kept fighting even when at death's door herself.

So she was proud of that one. If she ever stopped wearing her medals, the way Captain Brant had stopped when he returned home, she would keep wearing that one.

She rounded a corner and saw a gray work van parked across the street. Her skin prickled, and the hair on the back of her neck stood straight up.

She frowned. There was no reason to suspect that van, but her sense of danger existed for a reason. It had saved her life on more than one occasion, not the least of which was the instant before the Humvee rolled over the bomb, when she had a sudden feeling and shouted for her squad to take cover.

So, although logic suggested she was overreacting, she walked to the van and looked inside.

It was empty. The center console contained a half-empty pack of cigarettes, a lighter, and a water bottle. She walked to the back of the van and looked inside. The interior was lined with toolboxes and cabinets. A spool of copper wire sat in the upper right corner just behind the passenger seat.

She frowned and stepped back. There was a reason this van had alarmed her. Wasn't there?

She hesitated a moment, then got down on her knees and looked underneath the van. Nothing. No sign of an explosive device or tracking device. No hidden compartments and nothing suspicious at all.

She sighed and stood. Maybe it had been her imagination after all. Thinking about her injury had put her on edge. She shook her head and continued on.

She reached the bar a few minutes later. The others were there already, and when she walked inside, First Sergeant Orrin grinned at her. "Fashionably late as usual, Candy Girl."

"Kiss my ass, First Sergeant," she replied with a grin.

"Is that an invitation?"

She rolled her eyes and gave him the finger.

"Is *that* an invitation?" He asked.

"Unless your name is Ryan Geary and you're the sexiest auto mechanic on the planet, then no."

"I'll bet anything I can do better for you than he can."

"I guarantee you can't," she said as she made her way to the others.

This kind of banter might appall anyone who didn't understand the dynamic among the Platoon, but there wasn't anything serious behind it. First Sergeant would never dream of doing anything that would damage her relationship, and Candace would never dream of cheating on Geary, who in addition to being the world's sexiest auto mechanic and every bit as good in bed as she said was also the sweetest, gentlest human being she'd ever known. She'd always seen herself with another Marine when it came time to settle down, but there was something refreshing about a man who had no iota of violence within him. It made the violence she'd had to commit almost worth it.

The night wore on, and Candace lost herself in fellowship and brotherhood. Willy challenged her to a game of pool, which she won easily, and lamented that he should just leave the game behind altogether. First Sergeant made the mistake of telling everyone about the girl he'd been seeing for the past month and everyone made sure to rib him appropriately for it.

The only low point of the evening came when Sonny Boy talked about the plans for Owl's memorial. His body would rest at Arlington National Cemetery, but the memorial would take place right here in Pembroke.

"We're doing the main service at First Presbyterian," he said, "but Leah wants a private reception by Hoss Creek. Just her, the kids, and us."

"That's beautiful," First Sergeant said. "Count me in."

"What do you mean, count me in?" Smoke said, "Everyone's going to be there. It's Owl's memorial. No one's gonna miss that."

"How are the kids doing?" Candace asked.

Willy sighed. "Not so good. The older kids are okay. I mean, they're sad as hell, but they're being brave. But Cece's having a really hard time. Leah tells me that she wakes every night crying for her Daddy."

The others deflated at the news. Cece was only four years old, and they were all afraid that she would have trouble understanding that her Daddy was gone. Candace hated knowing they were right.

After a moment of silence, Smoke said, "Goddammit. I swear to God, if I ever see that asshole who killed Owl, I'm going to cut him up like a fucking sausage."

"You'll call us, and we'll all do him," First Sergeant said grimly. "That boy better pray to God those FBI agents find him before we do."

"Speaking of," Candace asked. "Have they found anyone yet?"

"I heard they've made a couple arrests, but nothing's definite yet," Sonny Boy replied. "Whoever this guy is, they want him for a few other murders, and according to my contact at Pembroke PD they're still trying to figure out a motive."

"Who gives a shit about a motive?" Willy asked. "Just find the guy and fuck him up already."

"They need a motive to find the guy," Candace said. "It's not like he left his calling card."

"Well, like I said," First Sergeant repeated, "He better hope the FBI finds him before we do."

They lapsed into silence again, each dealing with the grief of their most recent loss.

This time, it was Candace who broke the silence. "Hey, this is a good day. Owl would be pissed if he knew we were spending it moping about him." She lifted her glass. "To Owl."

"To Owl," the others echoed.

They drank, and Willy chuckled. "I can just hear him screaming and swearing at us from Heaven."

Sonny Boy laughed. "'What the hell is wrong with you? You're a Marine, right? Then stop whining like a little bitch and drink!'"

Smoke joined in on the laughter. "That sounds just like him."

"Sonny Boy should know," First Sergeant said. "He suffered more of Owl's wrath than any of us."

"Well, what did he expect?" Smoke said. "The number one rule of being a Marine is never get caught sitting on your ass."

The others continued to banter and trade stories about Owl, and Candace's mood slowly lifted once more.

The Owl was dead, but he wasn't gone. He would never be gone. Not as long as they were here to keep his memory alive. And when they were gone too, his spirit would join theirs and embolden the heart of everyone who took the oath and wore the eagle, globe and anchor.

They drank and played and bantered and talked and reminded themselves that they were still alive, still here, still brothers and sisters. Candace was the last one to leave, drinking in every moment of camaraderie she could. If she could keep having nights like this, then she could go on. Her purple heart still bled, but she could fight through it.

Finally, the First Sergeant admitted defeat. "Damn, Candy Girl," he said. "I never thought the day would come when a woman could drink me under the table."

"I'm not just a woman, First Sergeant," she reminded him. "I'm a Marine."

"Damn straight," he said. "Well, I should get on home before Julie goes off on me about being out drinking again. She's a good girl, but she's as close to a teetotaler as I ever hope to get. Best ass I've ever seen, though. Even better than yours, and that's saying something."

Candace chuckled. "Good luck with that, First Sergeant. I hope you get plenty of ass tonight."

"Oh, I will. You can bet yours on it."

She laughed. "I think I'll keep my ass to myself, but thank you for the offer."

He shrugged. "Your loss. I'll see you next time, Candy."

"See you later, First Sergeant."

She waited a few minutes longer, then finished her last drink and settled her tab. The bartender offered to drive her home, but she said she would call her boyfriend.She stepped outside to call, but before she could dial the number, a gloved hand reached around her and clamped shut around her mouth. Before she could react, the owner of that hand picked her up off of the ground and threw her into the back of the van—the same one she'd seen earlier. Dammit, she should have trusted her instincts.

She rushed forward, but the door slammed shut behind her, and whoever it was who had kidnapped her ignored her shouts as he walked to the front of the vehicle. She tested the panel door that separated the back of the van, but it was sturdy steel and reinforced with bars. It didn't budge as she kicked it and drove her shoulder into it.

The van started to move, and she fell backwards, barking her elbows on the hard steel floor. She grimaced and bit back a cry, then thought of her options.

The cabinets and drawers were all locked. The copper wire she'd seen earlier was gone. She had no choice but to wait until her kidnapper took her wherever he was going to take her and opened the door again.

*It's him*, she thought. *He's the one who killed Owl.*

Years of combat experience helped her control her physical reaction. She sat against the wall of the van and settled in calmly for the ride.

But that didn't quell her fear. Whoever this man was, he had killed Owl, and while Candace was supremely confident in her skillset, she knew that Owl was a better fighter in his sleep than she was on her best day.

And now his killer was taking her somewhere to deliver the same fate.

*Owl,* she thought. *If you're watching, I could really use a hand right now.*

# CHAPTER NINETEEN

Michael yawned and leaned back in his chair, rubbing his eyes. “Oy,” he said, “I’ll tell you what, whenever I do finally move on, these late nights are something I won’t miss.”

“I told you you could go back to the hotel and rest,” Faith reminded him.

“And leave you alone to have all the fun? Hell no.”

She smiled through her own exhaustion and said, “Well, if you’re going to be here, you can make yourself useful and go get us some coffee.”

“Hey,” he replied in an injured tone, “I am very useful. Ellie says I’m very handy.”

“Keep that between the two of you,” she teased.

“Don’t act like it’s not true,” he quipped. “You know it just as well as she does.”

“Seriously,” she said with a laugh, “Go get coffee or go get sleep before you say something you’ll regret.”

“I don’t regret anything,” he said, “If you do, that’s not my problem.”

“Go!”

Turk opened one eye and growled irritably. She ruffled his fur, and he closed his eyes again. "Sorry, boy. Michael and I are just going crazy."

He opened his eyes long enough to roll it, and Faith chuckled again.

It really was exhaustion that had her so giddy. Her mood wasn’t nearly as upbeat as she was acting.

The two of them had spent all night poring over the case, looking at it from every angle they could think of. Everything led them either in circles or to a dead end.

The victims were connected, but the connection was too vague. They were involved with the military either tangentially or directly.

It would have been helpful to find someone who was connected to all four victims, but they already had a man who fit that description in custody.

She looked out the window where the sun was starting to rise. In an hour or two, Aaron Blakely's lawyer would be here, and they would resume questioning.

Except that wouldn't happen. What would happen is that Blakely's lawyer would get him released and tell them that if they wanted to ask any more questions, they could formally charge him. Thus would begin a months-long or even years-long process of arraignments, indictments, investigations, discoveries and arguments before the case even went to trial, which would be another months- or years-long affair as both sides haggled over the jury, the evidence, and God only knows what else the legal system would conjure up.

Normally, Faith didn't have to handle any of that. She just did her detective work and let the attorneys and judges handle the legal side. If they couldn't find definitive proof of Blakely as the killer, however, she would become embroiled in the legal nightmare.

It wasn't the legal nightmare itself that she resented but the fact that she still wasn't sure Blakely was their killer. It just didn't fit, and whatever her dreams were trying to tell her, she didn't buy the assertion that order didn't matter. Things *always* made sense. What was missing was only the piece of the puzzle that made everything fit.

So what was that piece?

All of them were involved with warfighting, but only Jones and Murray had military backgrounds. The others interacted with the military, but they weren't veterans themselves. Only Murray was a criminal, but depending on your perspective, Duke and Montclair could also be seen as criminals.

Jones, however… She shook her head. She knew that there were people who hated military veterans, but she thought it was a real stretch to think that someone was just randomly killing people who were military veterans when every other victim had a scope of responsibility far greater than an infantry Gunny Sergeant.

It just made no sense.

She sighed and leaned back in her chair. She would have to give senselessness a shot. She couldn't keep banging her head against the same wall.

So what didn't make sense? That someone really was just targeting anyone involved in warfighting. That was ludicrous considering the disparity in involvement the victims represented, but Faith would humor the assumption.

So someone was angry at everyone involved in war and picked these victims. Why? Even random occurrences had some meaning, even if only to the person committing the actions.

All of the victims were in the Pembroke-Miller area. That suggested that the killer was also here. The gap between Murray and Jones represented a serious problem to their analysis, but it also suggested that the killer didn't live here, at least not full time.

A thought struck her then, hard enough that she nearly jumped out of her chair. Michael saw her reaction just as he walked in, and his eyes widened. "Got something?"

"The killer doesn't live here," she said. "We were right to notice that when we interrogated Henry Faulks. That yearlong gap between Murray and Jones wasn't empty. I'll bet you anything that more people died between him and Jones."

Michael nodded. "So what brought him back to town?"

"I'm not sure," she said, "but if we can find similar cases elsewhere, then we'll know where to look."

The two of them got to work, the coffee forgotten, their excitement more than making up for their exhaustion. Faith pored through the FBI database while Michael looked through other law enforcement databases.

Within minutes, they had hits. A former helicopter pilot in Mississippi, a manager of an arms' manufacturing plant in Wisconsin, the president of an NRA chapter in Louisiana, all murdered in a similar manner as their victims, but just different enough that the FBI hadn't flagged them as related to Murray's death. In two of the three cases, the word JUSTICE was written on their bodies rather than the word VENGEANCE above their heads, and though all victims had their throat cut, only the one with no word written had their arms sliced.

"Playing devil's advocate," Michael said, "I should point out that we can't really know for sure if these killings are related. It looks like New Orleans investigated the two JUSTICE deaths and created a profile of a crazed former soldier, but nothing ever came of that."

Faith thought about that for a moment. "That's not out of the question," she said.

"What? A crazed soldier?"

"Yes," she said. "It happens very rarely, but occasionally people come home and can't handle the silence after months or years of chaos and violence. Trauma and civilian life converge and send them over the deep end. It would explain why the victims are only loosely connected.

To us, they might as well be different people, but to a traumatized veteran, they're different faces of the same coin."

"But to go after fellow Marines?" Michael asked, "Assuming he is a Marine and not from one of the other branches. It doesn't make sense."

"Not to us," Faith agreed, "but to our killer, they're all guilty."

"But wouldn't he be guilty?" Michael asked. "If he was a soldier or a Marine too, then wouldn't he also be guilty?"

"Hmm," Faith said, "good point."

"Would there be anyone on a battlefield who wouldn't be 'guilty'?" Michael asked. "Someone who could honestly say that they didn't contribute to the deaths of others?"

She shook her head. "I don't know. Maybe the medics."

Both of them started at the same time. "The medics," Faith repeated.

"That explains the wounds," Michael said. "Surgical cuts like those you'd get from a scalpel."

"And positioned perfectly to cause the most damage to the blood vessels with the least damage to surrounding tissue," Faith added.

They quickly looked up VA offices for the sites of each murder and asked for information on doctors who had started there around the time of each killing and moved shortly after.

Time seemed to slow to a crawl as office after office professed no knowledge of such a doctor. Faith watched the minutes tick by and wondered if their killer was stalking another victim this very moment.

Finally, they called the VA in Rogersville, and got an answer.

"That sounds like Doctor Templeton."

Faith felt a rush of excitement. "Does Doctor Templeton have a first name?"

"Walter. He's a traveling physician who provides free surgical care to veterans around the country. He was at our VA when Murray was killed. I can't believe he would do something like that, though. He seemed so passionate about saving lives."

"In his mind, he might feel that his actions are saving lives," Faith said. "Can you tell me what his schedule has been for the past year?"

"Oh, he doesn't have a schedule. He's a volunteer, not an employee. He just goes where he wants to go."

"So you can't confirm his whereabouts?"

"I can confirm that he was here last year for six weeks and that he's been here for the past four weeks."

*Bingo.*

"You're telling me that Doctor Walter Templeton is at this very moment in your hospital."

"Well, not at this very moment, but he's been here for the past four weeks. He's taking today off, but he'll be in tomorrow, if you want to talk to him."

Before Faith could reply, she heard shouting outside.

"I don't give a fuck who you are! I want to speak to the Marine!"

Faith recognized that voice. First Sergeant Orrin Trask sounded pissed, but Faith had been around Marines enough to know that his anger hid real fear. She handed the phone to Michael so he could get Templeton's start time tomorrow morning and walked outside to see Sergeant Trask jamming his finger into the face of a frightened desk officer while three other police officers converged on him.

"It's all right," Faith called. "I want to hear what he has to say."

Orrin met Faith, and hope and relief came to his expression. "Sergeant Bold," he said, "Candy Girl's missing."

Faith's eyes widened. "Since when?"

"The last time anyone saw her was last night. She was at the bar with me and the platoon to celebrate the anniversary of our deployment. Her boyfriend called me this morning and said she didn't come home last night. He wanted me to check and see if she went home with anyone else—to sober up, I mean. She would never cheat on him. So I did, and no one's seen her.

"Has her car been found?" Faith asked.

Orrin shook his head. "Negative. She walked last night."

Faith felt the blood drain from her face. A moment later, the door opened again, and an imperious woman with dyed blonde hair and a pantsuit that was two sizes too small for her barged in. "All right," she shouted. "I want my client out of here, and I want him out now. If you assholes don't want to end up stuffing tacos for the rest of your life, you'll bring him out now."

"Release him," Faith told the officer. "Blakely's innocent."

The police officers looked at Faith in shock. Even the lawyer was shocked. Faith called Turk, and she, Michael and Turk left the stunned officers behind. Trask started after them, but Faith held her hand up. "We need to do this ourselves, First Sergeant. I know she's your girl, but we can't risk anything being complicated because you intervened. Call the unit together and have them check anywhere Candy Girl might have gone."

"I'll stay behind," Trask said, "but if we find Candy Girl, we're going in, Sergeant Bold, consequences be damned."

Faith knew better than to try to dissuade him. "Will you at least call me if you find anything?"

He nodded. "I will."

"Thank you."

The three FBI agents piled into the cruiser. Michael switched the lights and siren on and sped toward Rogersville. Normally, the drive would take an hour. With the lights and siren on and traffic headed the other direction, Faith hoped to reach the VA hospital in forty minutes.

She feared that it might be too late.

# CHAPTER TWENTY

Candace's eyes opened slowly. Her head swam, and it was a moment before she could remember what had happened the night before. She remembered being taken and thrown into a van. They had driven for an hour or so before they stopped. She waited for the door to open, and when it did, she launched herself at her attacker. They had struggled briefly, but the attacker had combat training, and he'd eventually overpowered her and knocked her out with a shot of sedative to her neck.

She groaned and waited for her vision to settle. She was in a room. It looked like a garage or a basement. She looked around. No garage door. A basement then.

She was in a chair, her legs and arms bound. She tested the chair and found it bolted to the floor. A gag was over her mouth, and her wrists and ankles were bound with extra knots. Her kidnapper had done an excellent job. She wasn't going to get out of this.

The door to the basement opened, and a man descended the stairs. Candace steeled herself and stared defiantly at him. If she was going out, she was going to go out like a Marine."

The man's face came into view, and Candace's defiant look melted into one of shock.

Him? No way. It couldn't be. Why was he doing this?

He smiled at her and said in the calm, gentle voice she remembered. "Good morning, Candy Girl. How are we feeling today?"

He reached forward and took the gag out of her mouth. She gasped and then, in a fit of rage, spit at him. His lip curled in distaste, and for a moment, she thought he was going to strike her.

Instead, he walked to that nearby workbench and grabbed a paper towel from the roll sitting on top of it. He carefully cleaned his face and said, "That was rude, don't you think?"

"It was you," she said, horror and grief vying for supremacy in her tone. "You killed Jones."

"I've killed many people," he said, "as have you. The difference is that I've only killed people who deserve to die."

“Doc,” she said, unable to believe that the platoon’s corpsman could be the serial killer who had taken Owl from them. “Why?”

He chuckled bitterly and turned back to her. “Why? For God’s sake, how far gone are you guys that you can’t even recognize the extent of your evil?”

“*Our* evil? Doc, you killed Owl! You killed our Gunny!”

“And I’ll kill every goddamn one of you,” he snarled, his calm disappearing in a mask of rage so pure it stunned Candace to silence. “Every one of you I can get my hands on.”

He walked closer and regained his calm. “This is the first time I’ve brought one of you here, but I figured it was time to be more cautious now that the FBI is on my trail. Would you believe that this house was for sale at less than a hundred thousand dollars? That’s a steal in any economy. I originally planned to just live off the grid here, but I suppose I’ll have to find somewhere else now. It’s irritating that I can’t make an example out of you, but at least you’re not living free while your victims are rotting in the ground.

“Victims? Doc, what the hell are you talking about? You’re the murderer!”

“So the people you killed overseas don’t count? The people you shot who were only fighting to protect their homeland from foreign invaders? Screw them, right? You alone have killed more than I have, probably more than I ever will, yet you call *me* the murderer. Is the executioner a murderer for letting the axe fall on the head of those who take innocent lives?”

“We were Marines, Doc. We were just—”

He crossed the distance toward her, pressing a scalpel to her neck, moving so quickly that she could barely register his speed. “I swear to God, if you say that you were just following orders, I’ll gut you and let you watch your intestines fall onto the floor, then pour bleach down your mouth so you can watch them burst!”

Candace fell silent, but shock still outweighed fear. She knew him. He was her brother. They had drunk together, fought together, laughed together. This was as shocking as if First Sergeant now stared at her with hate in his eyes.

He pulled away, and his thin veneer of calm returned once more. "I'm sure this is genuinely surprising to you," he said. "Owl looked just as surprised when he saw me. He didn't have a chance to verbalize it, of course. You should consider yourself lucky. You get to hear your sentence read. You have a chance to make peace with your God, although I can't imagine He's interested in your excuses. 'He who sheddeth man's blood, by man shall his blood be shed.' I forget what verse that is, but you understand my point."

“You travel the country performing free surgeries in VA hospitals,” she said. “I can’t understand how you could be the man who’s killing people one day and saving others the next.”

“Well, I’ll make it simple for you. I’m saving people one day and saving others the next. I’m even using the same tools.”

The thought that the same scalpel Doc used to kill Jones was the tool he used to fix up other suffering veterans made Candace's stomach turn. "I get the politicians and arms dealers," she said, "but why Barrett? Why Owl?"

“The same reason I shot Carter.”

Candace gasped. “Carter? You *shot* Carter?”

“I did. He wasn’t important enough that I needed to make an example out of him, and he was genuinely remorseful for his actions. I granted him an easy death and allowed him his privacy.”

Shock finally gave way to anger. “You asshole. You’re not a Marine.”

“Of course not,” he said, “I’m a Corpsman. A doctor. I save lives, I don’t end them.”

“So I’m not a life?”

“Not one that deserves to go on. You killed a lot of people, Corporal. You received a medal for killing people.”

He held up her Bronze Star, and she said, “Did you read my citation? I earned that medal for protecting a family of civilians. For *saving* life, not ending it.”

“You protected traitors who sold their homeland out for favors with the United States government. If it was a Russian soldier protecting an American family for selling state secrets to the Kremlin would you feel that Russian soldier deserved a medal.”

“That’s different!”

“Why? Because we’re the ‘good guys?’ I can’t believe you’re that naïve, Corporal.”

Candace shook her head. “How many?”

“Nine so far. You’ll make ten. I wasn’t planning on taking you. To be honest, after Montclair, I planned to end my stint at Rogersville VA and move on to Oregon. Then I saw you walking to the bar and decided I had time for one more.”

“You’re insane.”

"Your words mean nothing to me, Corporal. No more than the words of any murderer."

"You're going to meet justice, Doc. I promise you. You know the Platoon. You've taken three of us already. What do you think the others will do when they find you?"

"They didn't even suspect foul play after Carter's death. The FBI is fixating on the artist who was sleeping with the congresswoman I killed. They won't find me."

"The FBI agent is a Marine, Doc. She'll find you."

He chuckled. "It's always amazed me how arrogant Marines are. They're so certain they're invincible. As though getting through boot camp somehow makes them untouchable. I've *already* killed three of you. I won't have any trouble killing more."

"You're a piece of shit," she spat. "You worthless asshole."

"Your words mean nothing, Corporal. I've already said that."

He stepped closer and carefully affixed the gag again. "You know what? I'm going to make an example out of you after all. I'm going to hurt you. I'm going to think of ways to make you wish I had just shot you instead of leaving you alive. I can't kill you a hundred times for each life you've taken, but I can make you suffer enough for a hundred liftetimes."

He stepped away and grabbed his car keys. "I'm going to go get some supplies. Enjoy your last few hours on this Earth, Corporal. If I were you, I would pray for forgiveness. Your body belongs to me, but if God does exist, He might be persuaded to have mercy on your soul. Though I rather doubt it."

He left then, and Candace watched helplessly as he retreated up the stairs. He switched the light off, and just before he closed the door and plunged the room into darkness, she screamed, the gag muffling her cry and increasing her impotent rage.

# CHAPTER TWENTY ONE

Faith and Michael reached the hospital forty-five minutes after leaving the Pembroke PD police station. The receptionist's eyes widened when he saw Faith's expression.

"Can I help you?" he asked.

"We need to speak to Doctor Walter Templeton immediately," Faith said.

The receptionist blinked. "Um… okay. May I ask why?"

"We suspect him of murdering four individuals and kidnapping a fifth who he also intends to murder."

"Oh," the receptionist said. "Oh. All right. Um…"

He began tapping keys, his face flustered, and said, "Doctor Templeton isn't scheduled today. It looks like he's not coming in until tomorrow. Can I take a message? Or… I guess not."

"Take a breath," Faith said. "We need to know where he is."

"Well… I'm not sure how to find that information."

"He didn't leave an address for a hotel or a home he's staying in while he's in town?"

"Um… I don't think so. It's not coming up on his file."

Faith sighed. "Can I speak to his supervising attending?"

"Doctor Fowler isn't in today."

"Well," Faith said, forcing herself to stay calm and not overwhelm the already frazzled receptionist. "Can I have his number, please?"

"Doctor Fowler is a she."

Michael leaned over the desk, and the receptionist blanched at the intensity of his gaze. "Give us a phone number for someone who can tell us where to find the serial murderer who right now has his next victim in his grasp. Please."

"Oh, um. Okay. Okay."

The receptionist's hands trembled, but he managed to stay calm enough to get them a phone number. Faith immediately dialed it and when Doctor Fowler answered, she said, "Doctor Fowler, this is Special Agent Faith Bold with the FBI. We suspect Doctor Walter Templeton of serial murder. I need to know if he gave you an address or if you have any idea where he might be."

"What?" Fowler said. Then, sternly, "If you call this number again, I'll call the police."

"And if you hang up, I'll tell every newspaper in the country that you withheld vital information that could have saved a Marine combat veteran's life!" Faith snapped. "If you want to verify my ID, look up the phone number for the Philadelphia Field Office and give them my name. But do it after you give me an address for Doctor Templeton."

There was a brief pause on the other end. Then Doctor Fowler said, "Oh God. You're serious."

Faith threw the hand that wasn't holding the phone into the air. "Yes, I'm being serious!" she shouted. "For God's sake, tell me where the hell Walter Templeton is!"

"He's been staying at the Hilton Garden Inn," Fowler said in a far more subdued voice. "I didn't get a room number."

"That's good enough," Faith said.

She hung up and led Michael and Turk away from the shocked receptionist. As Michael sped toward the inn, Faith called ahead and got the room number.

And bad news. "He checked out yesterday."

She sighed but forced herself to remain calm and focus on what to do next. "Did he leave in a vehicle?"

"Yes. He was driving an old Chevy Express van. An early 2000s model, I think."

"Color?"

"Flat grey. It was a work van. He said he sometimes did traveling surgeries in places where there weren't any nearby hospitals and carried his tools in the van."

"License plate?"

"Umm… here, let me check."

The two minutes it took the concierge to look up the license plate were the longest of Faith's life. She tried to remain calm, but each passing second she could see the scalpel burying itself in Candace Rogers' heart.

"Okay," the concierge finally said. "I looked it up on the security camera. Ohio license plate TTW zero-two-one-five."

Faith wrote the number down and said, "Thank you."

She hung up and called the Rogersville Police Department. After a brief conversation with the receptionist to convince her that she was, in fact, from the FBI, she put an APB out on the van.

When she was finished, Matt asked. "Now what?"

She shook her head. “Now we look.”

“Where?”

She thought. “He would have to be somewhere removed from people to kill her and stage her without being caught. I think we drive outside of town and look through the farm-to-market roads.”

“All right.”

He switched the lights on and sped away from the VA hospital. As they drove away, he asked, “Do you think she’s still okay? The Corporal, I mean?”

Faith wished wholeheartedly that she could give a better answer than the one she gave. “No. Honestly, it’s probably too late for her.” She looked at Michael. “But we aren’t going to give up. Not until we see her body.”

Michael nodded. “I never thought I’d say this before, but I really hope you’re wrong.”

“Me too.”

***

By noon, they had traversed half of the farm-to-market roads, driving five miles out and back on each one and seeing no sign of Templeton. Faith’s hope for Candace had dwindled to a dim ember, but if they could at least catch their murderer before it was too late, then this would all be worth it.

“Come on,” she whispered. “Come on, you bastard.”

Her phone buzzed, and she nearly threw it out the window, answering it so quickly. "Bold."

“We have a hit on the van,” the officer said. “It was caught on a traffic camera leaving Rogersville heading west.”

We're sending units in that direction now."

“Good. What road was he on?”

“Looks like FtM three-eighty-two.”

Faith looked up and saw that FtM 382 was the intersection they were closing in on. She looked at Matt, and he spun the wheel, swerving West down the road.

“We’re on the road,” she said. “We’re four miles west of town. We’ll call you when we find the van.”

“Understood. Good luck, Agents.”

Faith hung up and leaned forward in her seat. Next to her, Turk stared out the window with similar intensity. She reached over and stroked his fur, allowing the contact to calm her and sharpen her focus. Matt gripped the steering wheel tightly but kept himself under control as they sped down the gravel road, eyes peeled for the van.

The gravel road turned to dirt after three miles. Five miles after that, the road continued as an unmarked trail that featured uneven terrain that forced Michael to slow down and navigate carefully so the police SUV didn't high-center on one of the many deep ruts.

"How did he get a van down here?" he asked. "Or should we turn around and try another way?"

"Keep going," Faith said. "He might have one of those all-terrain conversion kits that come with a lift and off-road tires. Those are popular these days."

"If he's not down this road, though, then we're taking ourselves out of the action."

"The police can handle one crazy person," Faith told him. "I'd rather cover every base, even the ones we don't think Templeton can reach. If they bring him in and not us, it's still a win."

"I know that," he said. "I'm not worried about the credit. I just don't want to lose him."

"We won't," Faith said, even though she had no way of knowing that. "It's only a matter of time."

The rough terrain forced Matt to drive at only ten miles per hour, and they moved with infuriating slowness. Faith did breathing exercises to calm herself, but each minute without sight of the van caused her anxiety to reach a fever pitch.

Finally, she saw a house in the distance. She pointed, and Michael said, "I see it. Can you see the van?"

She leaned forward and said, "No. We're still too far. Wait! Yes, I see it! It's parked behind the house!"

"Good deal," Michael said. "Call Rogersville PD and let them know."

She tried calling, but her cell phone had no signal. She tried the vehicle's radio but got only static.

"Dammit," she said when another attempt with her cell phone ended in failure. "Didn't we say we were going to get satellite phones?"

"I'll put a requisition in when we get back to Philadelphia," Michael said.

"Do you think they'll follow the road this far?" Faith asked. "The police?"

He shook his head. “I don’t know. If they know the house is out here, then yes, they’ll probably send a truck or two out this way. If they don’t, then… well, we’ll have to hope.”

They reached the house two minutes later, and quickly got out. Turk shot to the front door, and Faith said. "Go check the van, then meet us inside. Actually, come in through the back door. That way, if he tries to flee, we have both entrances covered."

“Got it,” Michael said.

He drew his weapon and rushed to the back of the house. Faith drew her own weapon and met Turk at the front door. “Easy boy,” she said, “I want us both coming home today.”

She knocked on the door and called, “FBI! Open up!”

Silence. As always. Would it kill the universe to have one of her criminals come out with their hands up and calmly submit to arrest? Just once?

She knocked again. “FBI! Walter Templeton! Open the door!”

No answer. She sighed. “Dammit. All right, Turk. Give mommy some room.”

Turk backed up dutifully, and Faith squared up to the door. She shifted her stance until she felt comfortable and took a deep breath. With a cry, she lifted her leg and kicked hard.

The door splintered easily. Faith took a brief moment to be thankful it was a cheap particle board entrance and not a solid hardwood model. In a previous case, their killer had been a huge, muscle-bound man who had broken through a solid maple door that weighed over two hundred pounds. Faith was in great shape, but she was not a muscle-bound hulk.

An eerie silence greeted her. A moment later, she heard the back door splinter, and Michael came around the corner.

The house was two stories, but a door to the right of the staircase appeared to lead to a basement. “You clear upstairs,” Faith said. “I’ll check the basement.”

“We should go together,” Michael said. “If he’s waiting down there, I don’t want you going in alone.”

“I won’t be alone,” she said. “I’ll have Turk.”

Michael frowned at her, but he didn’t protest. He knew better than to argue with her. He nodded and started up the stairs, handgun at the ready.

She tested the lock on the basement door. It was locked, of course. She squared up to it and found it just as flimsy as the front door. When it swung open, its latch shattered, she started cautiously down the stairs, Turk just ahead of her.

The light switch, thankfully, was just inside the door, so she was able to illuminate the staircase and the room below. Turk barked and rushed down the stairs, and Faith rushed after him.

Then she heard a thump, followed by a yelp from Turk.

“Turk!”

She rushed into that room and saw a chair sitting directly in the middle of it. Sitting in that chair was the bound form of Corporal Candace Rogers. She looked up at Faith with fear in her eyes and said urgently. “Behind you!”

She turned around just in time to see a leather baton heading straight for her head.

She didn’t feel the impact, but her vision burst into stars. She heard the thump of her body hitting the floor just as the world went black.

# CHAPTER TWENTY TWO

The first thing Faith became aware of was the throbbing in her head. She opened her eyes and found that her left wouldn't open all the way. Her forehead above felt swollen and thick. She lifted her hand to check the wound and found that it wouldn't move.

She tried to move her legs, and when they didn't move either, she realized she was bound. She forced her eyes open wider and saw that she was bound to a chair with her arms and legs tied together.

An image of the last time she was bound like this flashed through her mind. She saw Trammell's grinning face, smelled his sour breath, heard his lilting tenor voice, and a surge of panic coursed through her.

Her breathing quickened, coming in harsh gasps, and her vision swam as consciousness threatened to leave her once more.

"Breathe, Marine," a stern female voice said.

Faith looked to her left and saw Corporal Candace Rogers still bound where Faith had left her. Her shoulders were slumped, and her eyes were filled with exhaustion, but her head was held high and behind the exhaustion was the steely strength of a combat veteran.

"You're all right," Candace said. "You have a mild concussion, but nothing more serious than that."

Faith recalled the wet thump she heard just before she was hit. "Turk? My dog? Is he all right?"

Candace met Faith's eyes, and her expression told her all she needed to know. Grief and anger surged through her, and when she looked to her right and saw Turk lying motionless on the ground, blood on his face, the world spun around her. Her head flopped forward, and her breathing quickened again. "Oh God," she whispered. "Oh no. Turk. Turk!"

"Snap out of it, Staff Sergeant!" Candace barked. "We're in a bad spot here, and if we're going to get out of it, I need you focused."

Faith took a deep breath and called on the memory of her time in the Corps. "Understood, Corporal," she said crisply. "Did my partner attempt to intervene?"

"He's tied up behind us," Candace confirmed. "He heard you cry out when you got hit and came down after you. Doc hid just out of sight and hit him from behind." She looked toward the staircase, and her lip curled in contempt. "Because he's a fucking coward."

Faith turned around and saw Michael slowly blinking himself awake. "Doc as in Doctor Walter Templeton?" she asked.

"That's him. Traitorous bastard."

Faith's head ached, and her eyes had trouble focusing, but thanks to Candace's encouragement, she was thinking clearly again. "How long have we been out?"

"Fifteen minutes or so."

"Jesus," Michael groaned. "What the hell was that?"

"Sap," Candace informed them. "Heavy leather. He heard your car approach and waited for you down here. How did you find us?"

"We looked up similar cases around the country and linked them to Templeton," Faith said. "Then we got a description of his vehicle from the VA hospital in Rogersville and put out an APB.

Candace nodded. "Well, you did almost everything right, but you probably should have waited for backup."

"In hindsight, you're right," Faith said, "but I couldn't leave a Marine behind."

"I understand," Candace said, "I wouldn't have been able to stay away either."

"How long have you been down here?"

"He took me last night," she said. "I tried to escape when we arrived, but he injected me with a sedative. I woke up as you see me now. I don't know how long I've been here."

"What's he doing now?" Faith asked. "Where did he go?"

"He said he was going to drive the van up the road and leave it there as a decoy. I'm hoping that PD will meet him before he comes back."

Faith hoped the same thing. "Do you know what he plans to do when he returns?"

Candace met Faith's eyes and said drily, "Isn't it obvious?"

Faith sighed. "Yeah. I suppose it is."

"How far out were those police units?"

Faith shook her head. "Probably ten minutes."

Candace nodded. "Well, it's a safe bet they're not coming."

"You're correct," an unfamiliar voice replied.

Candace's eyes narrowed, and Faith followed her gaze to the staircase. A man descended slowly, and a moment later, Faith saw the smiling face of Corpsman Doctor Walter Templeton for the first time in the flesh.

It used to surprise her to meet serial killers and find that they looked just like any average individual. After over ten years with the Bureau, she no longer found that hard to believe.

But this case surprised her.

"You killed Marines," she said. "Why?"

"Do Marines have a special dispensation that immunizes them from death?" he asked.

"It's just unusual to see a Marine turn traitor," Michael said, making no attempt to hide his disgust. "It makes me think you were never really a Marine."

Walter chuckled. "If you mean to insult me by disavowing my connection to a gang of murderers, then you are quite of the wrong impression when it comes to my opinion of them."

"You're a coward, Doc," Candace spat. "You have us bound, and you're going to kill us when we can't defend ourselves."

"The pot and the kettle, Corporal," Walter said. "How many of your enemies could reasonably defend themselves? How many freedom fighters do you know who can stand toe-to-toe with an A-10 Warthog? It's not a fair fight."

"They struck the first blow," Candace argued.

"Did they? All of them? Every single person in the Middle East was responsible for nine-eleven? I have a hard time believing that, Corporal, and while there's little doubt that your value to the platoon was mostly as eye candy, I can't believe that you're foolish enough to believe it either."

"How about you untie me?" Candace suggested. "Then we'll see how much eye candy I am."

"You've twice tried to beat me physically and twice failed," Templeton replied smugly, "and in any case, I'm not here to get into a contest with you. I'm here to punish you."

"You're not going to get away with this," Michael warned. "They'll cut right through the bullshit. The safety net you've tied is too loose. I have faith they'll unravel everything you've done before too long."

Faith frowned at Michael's word choice. Have faith. Was that a message for her?

"Well," Templeton said. "You're not wrong about that. They know my name and face now, and once you three disappear, there will be no doubt that you were right. I'll have to flee to Canada. This is probably the end of my mission. It's annoying, but I always knew it would end eventually. I'm only one man. I can only make a small difference. My hope is that my small difference will lead to many other small differences which will combine to become a big difference. Maybe it won't happen until long after I've gone, but I can rest content knowing that I've contributed greatly to the end of war."

"You've rested all your hopes on loose threads," Michael said. "They'll fall apart right in front of you."

Loose threads. Loose net. Faith tested the ropes binding her wrists and found them considerably looser than before. As she pulled, they loosened even more.

"Little by little," Michael said, "the web you've woven will fray to pieces."

"My, what a poet we are!" Templeton said, smiling at Michael. "Your talents were wasted with the FBI. It's too bad you're realizing this too late to do anything about it. You might have been quite successful."

Faith continued to loosen the ropes, careful not to move too obviously and tip Templeton off. Candace glared at him and said, "You better pray to God the police find you before the platoon does. You know what they'll do to a traitor like you?"

"I imagine the same as I'll do to a murderer like you," Templeton said.

He walked to his workbench and reached for the scalpel. Faith's wrists came free, and Michael said, "Hello, officer."

Templeton's eyes snapped toward the staircase, and Faith reached down and quickly untied the ropes around her legs. Templeton chuckled. "Very funny, Special Agent. Maybe I'll cut you a new smile since you're such a..."

His words trailed off when he turned and saw Faith stepping out of her chair. He reached for his scalpel, and Faith rushed him.

She caught his wrist just before he brought the scalpel toward her. He was far stronger than her, and she knew she wouldn't survive toe-to-toe. So, she brought her knee up hard into his groin and slammed her elbow into his nose. He released a sound like a teakettle and stumbled backwards but kept a firm grip on the scalpel. Faith continued to pummel him with elbows and knees, desperate to incapacitate him before he could gather his strength.

But Doc didn't go down. Try as she might, she couldn't overpower him. With a cry of rage, he finally threw her off of him. She fell to the ground and rolled over just before he drove the scalpel into her eye. The blade snapped from the handle as it impacted the floor. It arced up and cut Templeton just above his eyes. A thin line of blood formed on his forehead, and blood began to trickle down.

He gasped in shock, and Faith brought her heel down hard on his shoulder blades. His nose hit the floor and shattered with a satisfying crunch. Faith dropped on top of him and reached for her handcuffs only to find that he had removed them when he'd knocked her out.

Her momentary delay allowed Templeton to reach behind himself and grab her wrist. With a grunt, he yanked her down onto the floor and rolled over so he straddled her. He snarled at her and moved his hands toward her neck.

Faith jammed her thumbs into his eyes, and he shrieked and reached for her wrists again. She bucked and brought her knee up hard into his back, forcing him to fall forward. When his hands came to the ground, she reached over one and pinned his elbow to her side. With a cry of effort, she slammed her opposite leg to the floor and rolled him over.

He anticipated the movement however and rolled with it, coming on top of her again. He brought his fist down hard into her jaw, and though she managed to bring her arm up to block the blow, it still reverberated through her skull.

He pounced at the advantage and brought his hands around Faith's windpipe. He squeezed hard, and Faith's airway was cut off. She opened her mouth and eyes wide and clawed at his face, but he ignored her and squeezed hard. She could feel her consciousness fading, and her movements grew weaker.

“Fight back, Marine!” Candace shouted. “Don’t you dare give up!”

“His head, Faith!” Michael cried. “Tear open his wound!”

Faith reached up and worked her fingernails inside the cut on Templeton's forehead. With every ounce of her fading strength, she pulled downward. His skin made a wet, tearing sound as it separated, and he made the teakettle shriek again and let go of her throat to claw at her hands.

This time, instead of rolling, Faith pushed his hips and worked her legs out from underneath. She got out from underneath him and grabbed the back of his head, then drove her knee into his temple with all her might.

He grunted and fell to the ground, then lay still.

Faith collapsed next to him, gasping with exertion. Her throat burned, and each breath sent fire through her lungs.

"We're not done yet, Marine," Candace said. "Untie us, and then you can rest. If he wakes up again, we'll handle him."

Faith forced herself to her feet and staggered to Michael. She untied him, and he immediately set to work binding Templeton. When she untied Candace, the Marine strode swiftly to Templeton, her eyes dark with anger.

"Stand down, Corporal!" Faith said, her voice coming out in a rasp. "We're Stateside, Rogers. The authorities will handle this."

Candace stared down at Templeton's prone body and said, "Or we can handle it right now. You two are the only witnesses. I'll do it if you need me to. You just need to tell them that it was justified defense."

"Can't do that, Corporal," Faith said. "We can't prove Templeton right. We're not murderers."

Candace's hands clenched into fists, but after a moment, she slowly relaxed them. Then she nodded and said, "All right. We'll do it your way, Staff Sergeant. But I want your word that he'll never have the chance to hurt anyone ever again."

"He won't," Faith promised. "He has at least seven victims that we know of, one of whom was a Congresswoman. He'll spend the rest of his life looking at the sun through a four-inch window."

Candace nodded. She breathed deeply and released it slowly. "All right."

Michael lifted Templeton's bound body and set him against the wall. "No cell coverage out here," he said. "Someone needs to drive back to civilization and let them know that we're bringing the murderer in."

"I'll do it," Candace said. "You two can take Templeton in the police cruiser."

With the situation handled, Faith focused on Turk, who still lay motionless in the corner. She rushed to his side and pressed two fingers to his neck, terrified at what the action would tell her.

"Come on, buddy," she whispered. "Please be okay."

She felt a pulse. It was weak and thready, but it was still a pulse. He was alive.

"Is there an animal hospital in Rogersville?" Faith asked.

"I think so," Candace said. "If not, there's one in Pembroke." She looked soberly at Turk. "I'm sorry about your dog. He's brave as hell. I'd go to war with him any day."

"Me too. He's a Marine just like us," Faith said.

"No kidding?" Candace said. "Well, that explains the bravery."

"He is brave," Faith said, tears welling in her eyes. "He's the best damned dog on Earth."

"He'll be okay, Faith," Michael said. He looked contemptuously at Templeton, who was groaning as he began to come around. "He's survived worse than this asshole."

Faith appreciated Michael's words of encouragement, but blood still trickled from Turk's head wound, and she worried that Turk might finally have met his match.

Dimly, she thought she could hear Franklin West laughing in the back of her mind. Cold rage coursed through her.

*I'll get you, you bastard,* she thought. *You can laugh all you want, but I'll get you.*

# CHAPTER TWENTY THREE

The surviving members of Platoon C, Bravo Company, 4th Battalion, 22nd Infantry Brigade, USMC, cheered as Faith and Candace entered the bar. Michael had stayed behind at the animal hospital with Turk but insisted that Faith join Candace. "I'll watch over him," he promised. "You need to go celebrate with your brothers and sisters."

She wanted nothing more than to stay at Turk's side, but she knew that Michael was right. Turk had suffered a skull fracture, and there was nothing they could do but wait. It would be better for her to take a moment to recover from her own mental wounds as much as she could so she could hold it together when she finally saw him.

So, after a tearful goodbye, she drove with Candace to the Happy House.

As soon as they walked inside, the others erupted with cries of "Ooh-Rah!" The two women were immediately surrounded. Hands clapped shoulders, stubbly lips pressed against cheeks, and other hands filled their hands with beers.

"Fuck yeah, Marine!" Smoke yelled, wrapping Faith in a bear hug.

"Badass bitches up in here!" Sonny Boy announced to the other, slightly alarmed patrons of the bar.

"Ooh-fuckin'-rah!" Willy announced.

First Sergeant snapped a crisp salute, and when Faith returned it, he snapped it down just as crisply.

"Taught that asshole a lesson!" Smoke said. "Hey, bartender! Get these Marines some drinks!"

The bartender smiled and set a pitcher on the counter. "On the house, Marines," he said.

"Fuckin-A!" Sonny Boy cried. He poured two more glasses with surprising deftness and handed one each to Candace.

Willy put his arm around Faith and pulled her close. "Sergeant Bold, I think I speak for all of us when I say that you are an honorary member of Platoon C now."

"Damn straight," First Sergeant agreed. "You earned your boots today, Marine."

Faith grinned. "I never took them off, First Sergeant."

The others cheered, and then they all erupted into a drunken, raucous and woefully off-key version of the Marine Corps hymn.

Faith worried about Turk terribly, but she found her spirits lift anyway. She had forgotten what it felt like to be with her brothers- and sisters-in-arms. When she joined the FBI, she allowed her time with the Corps to fade from her memory. She had suffered much overseas and hadn't found the strength to face it. After Trammell hurt her, any desire she had to reconnect had disappeared.

But now, as she sang and drank and laughed with her fellow Marines, she realized that she felt stronger than she had in years, since before she had ever heard of the Donkey Killer. She thought of what would happen if West came face to face with a group of people as loyal and brave as these. He'd be done for in a heartbeat.

After the initial greeting, the mood calmed, but only relative to the revelry with which it had started. At Candace's prodding, Faith played a round of pool with Willy, whose luck turned out to be every bit as bad as Candace promised. She won three rounds against him and used the sixty dollars she earned to buy another round of drinks.

"Now that's a real Marine right here!" Smoke announced as he lifted his drink. "Money is for beer and girls!"

"Or boys," Candace said, looking pointedly at him.

Smoke scoffed. "Look me in the eye and tell me that your boy toy gets a penny of your money, Candy Girl."

Candace shrugged and said, "All right. Good point."

They drank and laughed and played some more. When they tired of pool, they traded war stories. Faith told them all the story of getting caught by the platoon sergeant in a compromising position with another staff sergeant, they all roared with laughter.

"Damn, Bold!" Candace said. "Even I wasn't *that* foolish!"

"You sure you want to say that?" Orrin asked with a grin. "I could tell some stories you haven't shared."

The others whooped and Candace reddened. "Not unless you want me to tell some of the stories you haven't shared."

"Tell them," Orrin said, "I'm not ashamed." He sipped his beer and looked wistfully out at the night. I think about her every day."

"Go back to her," Smoke said. "I'm sure she's standing on her roof right now wishing you were in her arms showing her some good old American loving."

Sonny Boy chuckled. "She's probably in some other guy's arms wondering if she can charge extra for—"

“Finish that sentence at your peril,” Orrin warned.

“What sentence?” Sonny Boy asked innocently. “I didn’t say anything.”

Willy grinned at Orrin and said, “Owl would finish that sentence. Then he’d say a lot more sentences, and there wouldn’t be anything you could do about it.”

"Yeah, well, you're not Owl," Candace pointed out.

Their smiles faded as they reminisced about their fallen Gunnery Sergeant. After a moment, Faith lifted his glass. “To Owl. May he always look down at us and shout for us to get our damned shit together like Marines. Just like a good Gunny does.”

“Hell yeah,” Candace said reverently, lifting her own glass. “To Owl.”

“To Owl,” the others repeated.

They drank, and the evening continued with war stories about Owl and a few of Corporal Carter, the poor young man who hadn't even had a chance to see the face of his murderer. Faith stayed late into the evening, and when she left, the others embraced her and made her promise to visit.

“Count on it,” Faith said and meant it.

“Ooh rah, Bold,” Candace said, hugging her tightly.

“Ooh rah, Candy Girl.”

Candace declined the offer of a ride home. “I’d rather walk. I was going to walk the other night to honor Owl. I’ll be damned if I let a traitor take that from me.”

Faith nodded approvingly and embraced her new friend again. “I’ll see you on the other side, Marine.”

She drove to their hotel and checked out early, then drove to Rogersville where Michael waited with Turk. It would be a few days before he could travel, and when he came home, he would have to spend some time at the animal hospital in Philadelphia recuperating. The jury was still out on whether he would ever be able to work as a K9 again.

But he would live. Right now, that was enough for Faith.

Halfway to Rogersville, her phone rang. When the phone number came up on her dashboard, her eyes widened. She pressed the button on the steering wheel, and a familiar voice asked, “Faith? Is that you?”

Faith had endured more than her fair share of psychological distress over the past week. She had nearly lost her life for… hell, she didn't even know how many times now. She had seen her partner nearly die, been reminded viscerally of the sacrifices that her fellow Marines had made and still made, and watched as the broken body of her K9 partner and best friend was loaded into an ambulance and taken to a hospital for lifesaving surgery.

So when she heard David's voice over the speaker, she felt a relief so powerful it overcame her. She burst into tears and pulled to the side of the road so her weeping wouldn't cause her to crash. "David? Is that you? You're awake?"

"I'm awake," he said.

"For real? I mean, for good?"

"For real. I don't know if it's for good or evil yet, but I'll let you know when I figure it out."

She chuckled through her tears. "That's a stupid joke," she said.

"Well, yeah. If I started being funny all of a sudden, you wouldn't believe it was really me."

She laughed again. "That was better."

"Well, it's far from my best stuff, but in my defense, I am on some *really* good drugs right now."

She giggled, and the sound was so silly and innocent that she smiled through her tears. "Yeah, I made sure they gave you the good stuff. I know you're too straitlaced to accept if I handed them to you, so I didn't give you the choice."

"You strike me as an upper kind of a girl, not a pill-popper," he said.

"Are you kidding? Try to imagine me on meth or coke for a moment. I'd be a bigger problem than West."

"You're still a bigger problem than West. And from what Desrouleaux tells me, he's starting to realize that."

"You talked to Desrouleaux?"

"Yeah, he came to visit me to get my statement about West attacking me. I'm afraid I couldn't tell him much. I only remember waking up and seeing him standing in the corner."

Faith's smile faded as she remembered the damage West had done to him.

"Faith?" David said. "Hey, it's okay. I'm going to be okay. They're keeping me here for another week, but then I'll get to go home. And Desrouleaux is stationing agents by my house, so West isn't getting in again. This is all going to be over soon. The noose is closing. You'll get him."

"I know," she said. "I just…"

She stopped before she finished that sentence. She wanted now more than ever to tell David that she was done with the FBI, and she, Turk, and David should move away somewhere in the Midwest and live out their days fishing and fixing up cars and animals. They could buy some land and be happy and forget all about the cares of the world.

But West was still out there. Still hunting. Still obsessed with finishing the job that Trammell had started. As long as the Copycat Killer was at large, nowhere was safe.

"I know," David said softly. "One day, Faith. Sooner than you think. You just have a little more work to do. Then we can do whatever we want. Just stay strong. Keep in mind, Faith, that as hard as West has tried to break you, he still hasn't. I'm still alive. So is Michael. So is Ellie. So is Turk."

Faith gasped at Turk's name, and fresh tears fell from her eyes. David heard the cry and said, "Faith? Is something wrong with Turk?"

She took a shaky breath and said, "Um… He's in the hospital right now."

"Oh God," David exclaimed. "Did West get him?"

"No," Faith said. "It was another guy." She briefly summarized their case, finishing with the fight that she had had with Templeton in his basement.

"Damn," David said softly. "I'm so sorry."

"He'll be okay," Faith said. "He's got a long road ahead of him, just like you, but he'll be okay."

"That's good," he said. "How long do you have to stay out there?"

"A few more days. Just until the wound closes. His skull wasn't fractured, thankfully, so there's a low risk of complication. He'll have a nice new scar, though."

"Hell, it'll be an improvement. He'll look even scarier."

She chuckled. "Yeah, I guess so."

They talked for hours, sharing stories and reminiscing. Sometimes they just talked about nothing in particular. Faith drank up the sound of his voice, letting each sentence remind her that he was still here, he was still alive. When she closed her eyes, she could imagine that he was with her, his strong, kind arms wrapped around her, her head on his chest, listening to the strong rhythm of his heartbeat.

When she felt her eyelids grow heavy, she said, "Well, I should let you go. I have a half hour of driving left to do, and it's late."

"Of course," he said. "Just do me a favor and text me when you're not driving anymore so I know you're safe."

That little gesture of caring nearly overwhelmed Faith again. She clutched her phone to her ear and whispered, “I love you, David. I love you so much.”

“I love you too, Faith,” he said. “I’ll see you soon.”

“Bye, David.”

“Goodbye.”

When she hung up, she buried her face in her hands and wept again, but this time the tears healed her, purging away all of the fear and doubt and pain she’d felt ever since walking into David’s apartment and finding him hurt.

When her tears faded, she took a steadying breath and continue don her way. She was weary to her bones, but she remained alert until she reached the hospital. Then her fatigue finally overcame her, and she fell asleep curled up on the couch in Turk’s room. She felt strong arms wrap a blanket around her and murmured David’s name as she drifted off.

# CHAPTER TWENTY FOUR

Three days later, Turk was well enough to travel, but not by air. Michael rented an SUV, and they began the long trek back to Philadelphia. Faith sat in the back with Turk on her lap. He slept, breathing deeply, and Faith felt an ache as she looked down at his bruised body. He had lost weight in the hospital since he was rarely awake to eat and was fed mostly through IV. She was painfully aware of how old he was. At nearly nine years old, he wasn't especially aged for a dog, but he was near the retirement age for a K9 unit, and he wore his years of service hard.

Michael glanced at her in the rearview mirror, and Faith managed a smile. He returned a compassionate one of his own and said, "So I heard that David's getting released."

"Yes," she said, "he should be home when we get back to Philadelphia. Desrouleaux's going to have a few uniforms keep an eye on him."

Michael nodded. "Good. Anything from the units by your house?"

She shook her head. "No, and I doubt they'll see anything. I've done some thinking about West, and I've come to the conclusion that he's a coward."

He lifted an eyebrow. "You've only just now realized this?"

"I've only just now realized that he realizes this," Faith said. "I was so distracted by his MO and the fact that he hoodwinked me for months that I never thought to see things from his perspective."

"His perspective? Who gives a shit what his perspective is?"

She shrugged. "It might help me understand how to beat him if I think of things from his side. Anyway, I've thought, and I'm pretty sure that he's a coward and that he knows it. I'm equally sure that he'll never admit that to himself, but I think he knows deep down that he's ruled by fear. That's why he copied Trammell's MO. That's why he admires him so much. Trammell was insane and overconfident, but he wasn't a coward."

"His overconfidence is what did him in," Michael said. "He left too many signs for us to follow."

“Yes,” Faith agreed, “and West’s cowardice is what has allowed him to escape us for so long. But not forever.”

The SUV passed a sign that said WELCOME TO IDAHO.

Michael grimaced and said, “Hey, I know that you want to get home quickly, but do you mind if I detour South away from Granger? I’d just as soon never have to see that place again.”

“Fine with me. If I never enter another cave, it’ll be too soon.”

Granger, Idaho was home to a now-collapsed mine that had once housed a serial killer who murdered anyone who ventured into the cave system. The killer, the mine, and the town itself all seemed otherworldly, as though they had stepped out of normal reality into a strange parallel universe. Faith wasn’t superstitious, but thinking back on that little town made her wonder a little too much about what might lie underneath the Earth.

“Good,” Michael said, taking a junction onto a highway that would lead them a hundred miles away from the town and its eerie atmosphere.

They rode in silence a while longer, and when it became too oppressive for Faith, she asked, “How’s Ellie? Did you tell her we’re on our way home?”

Michael stiffened slightly, and Faith regretted the question. Before she could pull it back, though, Michael said, “Yeah, I told her. She’s… well. She still wants me to leave the FBI.”

“What did you tell her?”

He shrugged. “I told her that I want to eventually, but I can’t right now. She wasn’t happy with that response.”

"She understands, though, right?" Faith asked. "She knows why you have to do this."

“No one understands, Faith,” Michael said, and Faith could hear the exhaustion in his voice. “No one understands unless they take the same oath we take. It’s like Marines, I imagine. I could sympathize with what you went through, but I’ll never really understand, will I?”

“No,” Faith admitted. “Not unless you were there with us.”

“Well, it’s the same with the FBI,” he said. “Any job like ours, really. We choose to live on the edge of darkness so that darkness doesn’t spill into the light. People who live only in the light never get to see that darkness, so how can they understand why we can’t look away?”

“But Ellie’s seen it,” Faith insisted. “She was married to it for twelve years.”

"Love is blind, Faith," Michael replied. "I think I'm starting to understand exactly what that means."

They lapsed into silence again, and this time the silence remained unbroken for the next several hours. Faith looked out the window and watched the landscape fly by while her dog breathed steadily in her arms.

Love was blind at times, she agreed. At other times, it saw clearly and simply chose not to look.

Sometimes knowing was worse.

***

Faith promised herself she wouldn't cry when she saw David, but as soon as he greeted her with the dazzling smile that had won her heart over a year ago, the floodgates opened. She buried her head in his shoulder and allowed everything to flow out of her.

She clung to him, breathing deeply of him, hearing his voice tell her everything was all right, feeling his arms around her, believing that he was here, he was hers, and he was safe. And as long as he was safe, so was she.

When her tears dried, they talked. "How are you feeling?"

"Well, my hands shake a bit, but the doctors say that's temporary. A few weeks eating solid food and moving around, and they say it'll calm down. I can go back to work in a month. How's Turk?"

"Better every day," she said. "He's going to be at the animal hospital for a few weeks, but he'll be released home after that."

"Will he work again?"

Faith sighed. "I don't know. The doctors won't give me a straight answer, but they wouldn't give me a straight answer when I asked if you would ever wake up, and here you are, so I haven't lost hope."

"That's good," he said. "You shouldn't. That dog's tougher than you, and we both know that's saying a lot. He'll pull through."

Faith smiled. "Yeah. I think you're right."

Her smile faded slightly, and David asked. "How are *you* doing?"

She sighed and weighed her response, but she didn't have to weigh it for long. She had come too close to losing David to want to lie to him anymore.

"I'm all right," she said, "but… I'm thinking about retiring."

"After West?"

"Yes," she said, "after West."

He nodded. "Well, I will support you no matter what you decide, but whatever happens, Faith, make sure it's because it's what you want to do, not because it's what you think you have to do. I know you and I have had differences in the past about your work, but I don't feel that way anymore. What you do is important, and if it fulfills you, you should keep doing it."

She smiled at him and said, "I know. I just don't know if it fulfills me anymore. Lately, I'm relieved when a case is done, and I can have a break from the violence and pain. I don't know yet if it's just exhaustion or if my heart just isn't in this anymore."

David smiled and caressed her cheek. "If you do walk away, walk away with your head held high. You did good, Faith. You should be proud of yourself."

She nodded. "I wish that was enough."

"Make it enough," he said. "Your demons don't deserve to haunt you."

She smiled and kissed the tip of his nose. "That was cheesy and adorable."

"That's me," he replied with a smile of his own. "That's why you love me."

"Yes," she agreed. "That's exactly why I love you."

"And I love you," he replied. "Come on. Let's go see Turk before visiting hours are over."

They arrived at the animal hospital an hour before visiting hours closed. Turk barked joyfully when he saw them, but instead of running up and jumping at them like he usually did, he carefully stepped his way to them, favoring each of his limbs as though riddled with the arthritis of a dog half again his age.

Faith forced the pain away from her heart and bent low to hug him. David knelt down, too, and when she saw him grimace at the effort, tears came to her eyes. Too many of the people in her life had been hurt. She was tired of watching them suffer.

But they were still here. West's best efforts hadn't been enough to take them from her.

She saw someone approaching and stood to see Special Agent Desrouleaux smiling sadly at her. He held out his hand, and she pulled him into an embrace. "Hi, Desi," she said.

"Desi?" he chuckled. "I haven't heard that name in a while. You okay?"

“I’ve been better,” she admitted. She turned back to Turk and David, who smiled and talked as though they understood every word the other said. “But I’ve been worse.”

“Yeah,” Desrouleaux agreed. “I feel you. Nice for the good guys to win a few, eh?”

She nodded in agreement.

“So I’m putting four agents here and four at David’s apartment. I’m putting six at your place, the four guards and me and Chavez. We’ll stay out of your hair, but we still think you’re the primary target, so I want to be there if Assface makes his way back into the light.”

Faith was almost certain that he would stay away from the light until the beam faced elsewhere, but she nodded and said, “Thank you.”

“Don’t mention it. You’d do the same for me.”

They watched Turk and David for a moment. David tossed a ball gently, and Turk trotted carefully to retrieve it, then brought it back.

“You ever think about Gordon?” Desrouleaux asked.

“All the time,” Faith said.

Special Agent Gordon Clark was a friend and mentor of Faith's and, for a time, her supervisor. He had been attacked in his apartment by West just before Faith learned the true identity of the Copycat Killer. Unlike David, he wasn't lucky enough to survive.

“Me too. I keep thinking of something he told me, that the rats we fight seem dangerous to us because we’re hunting them, but thanks to our efforts, the world at large never even knows they exist. I used to hang on those words.”

“Me too.”

“Now, though,” he shook his head. “I don’t know. With West’s face all over the news and him making us look like fools, I’m beginning to think that some of these rats might be too big for us.”

"No," Faith said. "Big, but not too big. Never too big. You and I are standing in a public room in a public hospital, showing our actual faces and using our actual names. We're going to drive home without having to worry that someone might recognize us and turn us in for money. West has to hide in the sewers, and even if he manages to bite a few throats, he'll never be anything more than a rat in the sewers. He can't win. All he can do is annoy us. Eventually, he won't be able to do that anymore."

Desrouleaux chuckled. “That’s why I like you, Faith. You can get kicked and beaten and stomped from here to high Heaven and low Hell, and you still come out of it with a smile on your face. No wonder Gordon liked you so much."

"That's the job, isn't it?" she said. "Keep smiling through the pain and keep putting the bad guys away."

"Yep," Desrouleaux agreed. "God bless the FBI."

They fell silent and watched Turk and David play until the veterinary nurse gently informed them that visiting hours were over. Faith rode home with David, and when they reached her apartment, she showed him in the most powerful way how alive he really was.

As she drifted to sleep in his arms, she smiled. That night, Dr. West remained hidden in the sewers and Jethro Trammell remained hidden in the grave, and her sleep was untroubled by nightmares.

# EPILOGUE

Across the street from the animal hospital, Dr. West sat in his car. He was parked over a sewer grate, but he didn't realize it. His attention was focused on the hospital ahead, more specifically a certain German Shepherd that recuperated within its walls. Four deadly serious FBI agents guarded him, and as confident as West was in his fighting skill, he knew he had no chance of reaching Turk while they were there.

But that wouldn't stop him. He would find a way inside. There was always a way.

Faith should have stayed with Turk. Visiting hours be damned, she should have forced herself by his side and raised hell until they relented. She could keep West from hurting Turk if she wanted, although not without help from the other four agents.

These four without Faith, though were weak. They were like pawns, able to do a serviceable job but not more than that. Faith was a queen, able to move anywhere with very few limitations. She had done herself and Turk a disservice by heading home.

Then again, she hadn't seen her boyfriend in a while, and she had needs too. His lip curled in disgust. People were so predictable. He hated the fact that that included Faith.

He watched the hospital for a while but eventually drove on. He couldn't get in tonight. Probably not for several nights.

He would get in, though. He would find Turk, and this time, the dog would be too weak to fight back the way it had in Faiths' apartment.

He grinned as he thought of throttling the life out of that damned mutt and the look on Faith's face when she realized that no protection was enough to stop him. He would take his pound of flesh, and Faith would know once and for all that he was too much for her to handle.

And if that didn't break her, he would do the same with David. And Michael. And everyone she knew and loved. Faith Bold belonged to him. She just refused to admit it.

But not forever. Of that, he would make sure.

## NOW AVAILABLE!

### SO CRUEL
### (A Faith Bold Mystery—Book 13)

**When the world of unethical dog-breeding turns deadly, the case becomes personal for FBI Agent Faith Bold and her loyal canine. Together, they must track down a ruthless killer before he strikes again…**

"A masterpiece of thriller and mystery."
—Books and Movie Reviews, Roberto Mattos (re Once Gone)

SO CRUEL is Book #13 in a long-anticipated new series by #1 bestseller and USA Today bestselling author Blake Pierce, whose bestseller Once Gone (a free download) has received over 7,000 five star ratings and reviews.

FBI Special Agent Faith Bold doesn't believe she can ever return to the force after the trauma she's been through. Suffering from past demons, she feels unfit for duty and content to retire—until Turk walks into her life.

Turk, a former Marine Corps dog, wounded in battle, suffers from his own demons. But he never lets it show as he gives everything to Faith to get her back on her feet.

Each are slow to warm up to each other, but when they do, they are inseparable. Each is equally determined to hunt down the demons chasing them, whatever the cost, and to watch each other's backs—even at the risk of their own life.

A page-turning and harrowing crime thriller featuring a brilliant and tortured FBI agent, the Faith Bold series is a riveting mystery, packed with non-stop action, suspense, twists and turns, revelations, and driven by a breakneck pace that will keep you flipping pages late into the night. Fans of Rachel Caine, Teresa Driscoll and Robert Dugoni are sure to fall in love.

Future books in the series are now also available.

“An edge of your seat thriller in a new series that keeps you turning pages! ...So many twists, turns and red herrings… I can't wait to see what happens next.”
—Reader review (Her Last Wish)

“A strong, complex story about two FBI agents trying to stop a serial killer. If you want an author to capture your attention and have you guessing, yet trying to put the pieces together, Pierce is your author!”
—Reader review (Her Last Wish)

“A typical Blake Pierce twisting, turning, roller coaster ride suspense thriller. Will have you turning the pages to the last sentence of the last chapter!!!”
—Reader review (City of Prey)

“Right from the start we have an unusual protagonist that I haven't seen done in this genre before. The action is nonstop… A very atmospheric novel that will keep you turning pages well into the wee hours.”
—Reader review (City of Prey)

“Everything that I look for in a book… a great plot, interesting characters, and grabs your interest right away. The book moves along at a breakneck pace and stays that way until the end. Now on go I to book two!”
—Reader review (Girl, Alone)

“Exciting, heart pounding, edge of your seat book… a must read for mystery and suspense readers!”
—Reader review (Girl, Alone)

**Blake Pierce**

Blake Pierce is the USA Today bestselling author of the RILEY PAGE mystery series, which includes seventeen books. Blake Pierce is also the author of the MACKENZIE WHITE mystery series, comprising fourteen books; of the AVERY BLACK mystery series, comprising six books; of the KERI LOCKE mystery series, comprising five books; of the MAKING OF RILEY PAIGE mystery series, comprising six books; of the KATE WISE mystery series, comprising seven books; of the CHLOE FINE psychological suspense mystery, comprising six books; of the JESSIE HUNT psychological suspense thriller series, comprising thirty-five books (and counting); of the AU PAIR psychological suspense thriller series, comprising three books; of the ZOE PRIME mystery series, comprising six books; of the ADELE SHARP mystery series, comprising sixteen books, of the EUROPEAN VOYAGE cozy mystery series, comprising six books; of the LAURA FROST FBI suspense thriller, comprising eleven books; of the ELLA DARK FBI suspense thriller, comprising twenty-one books (and counting); of the A YEAR IN EUROPE cozy mystery series, comprising nine books, of the AVA GOLD mystery series, comprising six books; of the RACHEL GIFT mystery series, comprising fifteen books (and counting); of the VALERIE LAW mystery series, comprising nine books; of the PAIGE KING mystery series, comprising eight books; of the MAY MOORE mystery series, comprising eleven books; of the CORA SHIELDS mystery series, comprising eight books; of the NICKY LYONS mystery series, comprising eight books, of the CAMI LARK mystery series, comprising ten books; of the AMBER YOUNG mystery series, comprising seven books (and counting); of the DAISY FORTUNE mystery series, comprising five books; of the FIONA RED mystery series, comprising eleven books (and counting); of the FAITH BOLD mystery series, comprising fourteen books (and counting); of the JULIETTE HART mystery series, comprising five books (and counting); of the MORGAN CROSS mystery series, comprising ten books (and counting); of the FINN WRIGHT mystery series, comprising six books (and counting); of the new SHEILA STONE suspense thriller series, comprising five books (and counting); and of the new RACHEL BLACKWOOD suspense thriller series, comprising five books (and counting).

An avid reader and lifelong fan of the mystery and thriller genres, Blake loves to hear from you, so please feel free to visit www.blakepierceauthor.com to learn more and stay in touch.

## BOOKS BY BLAKE PIERCE

**RACHEL BLACKWOOD SUSPENSE THRILLER**

NOT THIS WAY (Book #1)
NOT THIS TIME (Book #2)
NOT THIS CLOSE (Book #3)
NOT THIS ROAD (Book #4)
NOT THIS LATE (Book #5)

**SHEILA STONE SUSPENSE THRILLER**

SILENT GIRL (Book #1)
SILENT TRAIL (Book #2)
SILENT NIGHT (Book #3)
SILENT HOUSE (Book #4)
SILENT SCREAM (Book #5)

**FINN WRIGHT MYSTERY SERIES**

WHEN YOU'RE MINE (Book #1)
WHEN YOU'RE SAFE (Book #2)
WHEN YOU'RE CLOSE (Book #3)
WHEN YOU'RE SLEEPING (Book #4)
WHEN YOU'RE SANE (Book #5)
WHEN YOU'RE SILENT (Book #6)

**MORGAN CROSS MYSTERY SERIES**

FOR YOU (Book #1)
FOR RAGE (Book #2)
FOR LUST (Book #3)
FOR WRATH (Book #4)
FOREVER (Book #5)
FOR US (Book #6)
FOR NOW (Book #7)
FOR ONCE (Book #8)
FOR ETERNITY (Book #9)
FORLORN (Book #10)

**JULIETTE HART MYSTERY SERIES**

NOTHING TO FEAR (Book #1)
NOTHING THERE (Book #2)
NOTHING WATCHING (Book #3)
NOTHING HIDING (Book #4)
NOTHING LEFT (Book #5)

**FAITH BOLD MYSTERY SERIES**
SO LONG (Book #1)
SO COLD (Book #2)
SO SCARED (Book #3)
SO NORMAL (Book #4)
SO FAR GONE (Book #5)
SO LOST (Book #6)
SO ALONE (Book #7)
SO FORGOTTEN (Book #8)
SO INSANE (Book #9)
SO SMITTEN (Book #10)
SO SIMPLE (Book #11)
SO BROKEN (Book #12)
SO CRUEL (Book #13)
SO HAUNTED (Book #14)

**FIONA RED MYSTERY SERIES**
LET HER GO (Book #1)
LET HER BE (Book #2)
LET HER HOPE (Book #3)
LET HER WISH (Book #4)
LET HER LIVE (Book #5)
LET HER RUN (Book #6)
LET HER HIDE (Book #7)
LET HER BELIEVE (Book #8)
LET HER FORGET (Book #9)
LET HER TRY (Book #10)
LET HER PLAY (Book #11)

**DAISY FORTUNE MYSTERY SERIES**
NEED YOU (Book #1)
CLAIM YOU (Book #2)
CRAVE YOU (Book #3)
CHOOSE YOU (Book #4)

CHASE YOU (Book #5)

**AMBER YOUNG MYSTERY SERIES**
ABSENT PITY (Book #1)
ABSENT REMORSE (Book #2)
ABSENT FEELING (Book #3)
ABSENT MERCY (Book #4)
ABSENT REASON (Book #5)
ABSENT SANITY (Book #6)
ABSENT LIFE (Book #7)

**CAMI LARK MYSTERY SERIES**
JUST ME (Book #1)
JUST OUTSIDE (Book #2)
JUST RIGHT (Book #3)
JUST FORGET (Book #4)
JUST ONCE (Book #5)
JUST HIDE (Book #6)
JUST NOW (Book #7)
JUST HOPE (Book #8)
JUST LEAVE (Book #9)
JUST TONIGHT (Book #10)

**NICKY LYONS MYSTERY SERIES**
ALL MINE (Book #1)
ALL HIS (Book #2)
ALL HE SEES (Book #3)
ALL ALONE (Book #4)
ALL FOR ONE (Book #5)
ALL HE TAKES (Book #6)
ALL FOR ME (Book #7)
ALL IN (Book #8)

**CORA SHIELDS MYSTERY SERIES**
UNDONE (Book #1)
UNWANTED (Book #2)
UNHINGED (Book #3)
UNSAID (Book #4)
UNGLUED (Book #5)
UNSTABLE (Book #6)

UNKNOWN (Book #7)
UNAWARE (Book #8)

**MAY MOORE SUSPENSE THRILLER**
NEVER RUN (Book #1)
NEVER TELL (Book #2)
NEVER LIVE (Book #3)
NEVER HIDE (Book #4)
NEVER FORGIVE (Book #5)
NEVER AGAIN (Book #6)
NEVER LOOK BACK (Book #7)
NEVER FORGET (Book #8)
NEVER LET GO (Book #9)
NEVER PRETEND (Book #10)
NEVER HESITATE (Book #11)

**PAIGE KING MYSTERY SERIES**
THE GIRL HE PINED (Book #1)
THE GIRL HE CHOSE (Book #2)
THE GIRL HE TOOK (Book #3)
THE GIRL HE WISHED (Book #4)
THE GIRL HE CROWNED (Book #5)
THE GIRL HE WATCHED (Book #6)
THE GIRL HE WANTED (Book #7)
THE GIRL HE CLAIMED (Book #8)

**VALERIE LAW MYSTERY SERIES**
NO MERCY (Book #1)
NO PITY (Book #2)
NO FEAR (Book #3)
NO SLEEP (Book #4)
NO QUARTER (Book #5)
NO CHANCE (Book #6)
NO REFUGE (Book #7)
NO GRACE (Book #8)
NO ESCAPE (Book #9)

**RACHEL GIFT MYSTERY SERIES**
HER LAST WISH (Book #1)
HER LAST CHANCE (Book #2)

HER LAST HOPE (Book #3)
HER LAST FEAR (Book #4)
HER LAST CHOICE (Book #5)
HER LAST BREATH (Book #6)
HER LAST MISTAKE (Book #7)
HER LAST DESIRE (Book #8)
HER LAST REGRET (Book #9)
HER LAST HOUR (Book #10)
HER LAST SHOT (Book #11)
HER LAST PRAYER (Book #12)
HER LAST LIE (Book #13)
HER LAST WHISPER (Book #14)
HER LAST SECRET (Book #15)

**AVA GOLD MYSTERY SERIES**
CITY OF PREY (Book #1)
CITY OF FEAR (Book #2)
CITY OF BONES (Book #3)
CITY OF GHOSTS (Book #4)
CITY OF DEATH (Book #5)
CITY OF VICE (Book #6)

**A YEAR IN EUROPE**
A MURDER IN PARIS (Book #1)
DEATH IN FLORENCE (Book #2)
VENGEANCE IN VIENNA (Book #3)
A FATALITY IN SPAIN (Book #4)

**ELLA DARK FBI SUSPENSE THRILLER**
GIRL, ALONE (Book #1)
GIRL, TAKEN (Book #2)
GIRL, HUNTED (Book #3)
GIRL, SILENCED (Book #4)
GIRL, VANISHED (Book 5)
GIRL ERASED (Book #6)
GIRL, FORSAKEN (Book #7)
GIRL, TRAPPED (Book #8)
GIRL, EXPENDABLE (Book #9)
GIRL, ESCAPED (Book #10)
GIRL, HIS (Book #11)

GIRL, LURED (Book #12)
GIRL, MISSING (Book #13)
GIRL, UNKNOWN (Book #14)
GIRL, DECEIVED (Book #15)
GIRL, FORLORN (Book #16)
GIRL, REMADE (Book #17)
GIRL, BETRAYED (Book #18)
GIRL, BOUND (Book #19)
GIRL, REFORMED (Book #20)
GIRL, REBORN (Book #21)

**LAURA FROST FBI SUSPENSE THRILLER**
ALREADY GONE (Book #1)
ALREADY SEEN (Book #2)
ALREADY TRAPPED (Book #3)
ALREADY MISSING (Book #4)
ALREADY DEAD (Book #5)
ALREADY TAKEN (Book #6)
ALREADY CHOSEN (Book #7)
ALREADY LOST (Book #8)
ALREADY HIS (Book #9)
ALREADY LURED (Book #10)
ALREADY COLD (Book #11)

**EUROPEAN VOYAGE COZY MYSTERY SERIES**
MURDER (AND BAKLAVA) (Book #1)
DEATH (AND APPLE STRUDEL) (Book #2)
CRIME (AND LAGER) (Book #3)
MISFORTUNE (AND GOUDA) (Book #4)
CALAMITY (AND A DANISH) (Book #5)
MAYHEM (AND HERRING) (Book #6)

**ADELE SHARP MYSTERY SERIES**
LEFT TO DIE (Book #1)
LEFT TO RUN (Book #2)
LEFT TO HIDE (Book #3)
LEFT TO KILL (Book #4)
LEFT TO MURDER (Book #5)
LEFT TO ENVY (Book #6)
LEFT TO LAPSE (Book #7)

LEFT TO VANISH (Book #8)
LEFT TO HUNT (Book #9)
LEFT TO FEAR (Book #10)
LEFT TO PREY (Book #11)
LEFT TO LURE (Book #12)
LEFT TO CRAVE (Book #13)
LEFT TO LOATHE (Book #14)
LEFT TO HARM (Book #15)
LEFT TO RUIN (Book #16)

**THE AU PAIR SERIES**
ALMOST GONE (Book#1)
ALMOST LOST (Book #2)
ALMOST DEAD (Book #3)

**ZOE PRIME MYSTERY SERIES**
FACE OF DEATH (Book#1)
FACE OF MURDER (Book #2)
FACE OF FEAR (Book #3)
FACE OF MADNESS (Book #4)
FACE OF FURY (Book #5)
FACE OF DARKNESS (Book #6)

**A JESSIE HUNT PSYCHOLOGICAL SUSPENSE SERIES**
THE PERFECT WIFE (Book #1)
THE PERFECT BLOCK (Book #2)
THE PERFECT HOUSE (Book #3)
THE PERFECT SMILE (Book #4)
THE PERFECT LIE (Book #5)
THE PERFECT LOOK (Book #6)
THE PERFECT AFFAIR (Book #7)
THE PERFECT ALIBI (Book #8)
THE PERFECT NEIGHBOR (Book #9)
THE PERFECT DISGUISE (Book #10)
THE PERFECT SECRET (Book #11)
THE PERFECT FAÇADE (Book #12)
THE PERFECT IMPRESSION (Book #13)
THE PERFECT DECEIT (Book #14)
THE PERFECT MISTRESS (Book #15)
THE PERFECT IMAGE (Book #16)

THE PERFECT VEIL (Book #17)
THE PERFECT INDISCRETION (Book #18)
THE PERFECT RUMOR (Book #19)
THE PERFECT COUPLE (Book #20)
THE PERFECT MURDER (Book #21)
THE PERFECT HUSBAND (Book #22)
THE PERFECT SCANDAL (Book #23)
THE PERFECT MASK (Book #24)
THE PERFECT RUSE (Book #25)
THE PERFECT VENEER (Book #26)
THE PERFECT PEOPLE (Book #27)
THE PERFECT WITNESS (Book #28)
THE PERFECT APPEARANCE (Book #29)
THE PERFECT TRAP (Book #30)
THE PERFECT EXPRESSION (Book #31)
THE PERFECT ACCOMPLICE (Book #32)
THE PERFECT SHOW (Book #33)
THE PERFECT POISE (Book #34)
THE PERFECT CROWD (Book #35)

**CHLOE FINE PSYCHOLOGICAL SUSPENSE SERIES**

NEXT DOOR (Book #1)
A NEIGHBOR'S LIE (Book #2)
CUL DE SAC (Book #3)
SILENT NEIGHBOR (Book #4)
HOMECOMING (Book #5)
TINTED WINDOWS (Book #6)

**KATE WISE MYSTERY SERIES**

IF SHE KNEW (Book #1)
IF SHE SAW (Book #2)
IF SHE RAN (Book #3)
IF SHE HID (Book #4)
IF SHE FLED (Book #5)
IF SHE FEARED (Book #6)
IF SHE HEARD (Book #7)

**THE MAKING OF RILEY PAIGE SERIES**

WATCHING (Book #1)
WAITING (Book #2)

LURING (Book #3)
TAKING (Book #4)
STALKING (Book #5)
KILLING (Book #6)

**RILEY PAIGE MYSTERY SERIES**
ONCE GONE (Book #1)
ONCE TAKEN (Book #2)
ONCE CRAVED (Book #3)
ONCE LURED (Book #4)
ONCE HUNTED (Book #5)
ONCE PINED (Book #6)
ONCE FORSAKEN (Book #7)
ONCE COLD (Book #8)
ONCE STALKED (Book #9)
ONCE LOST (Book #10)
ONCE BURIED (Book #11)
ONCE BOUND (Book #12)
ONCE TRAPPED (Book #13)
ONCE DORMANT (Book #14)
ONCE SHUNNED (Book #15)
ONCE MISSED (Book #16)
ONCE CHOSEN (Book #17)

**MACKENZIE WHITE MYSTERY SERIES**
BEFORE HE KILLS (Book #1)
BEFORE HE SEES (Book #2)
BEFORE HE COVETS (Book #3)
BEFORE HE TAKES (Book #4)
BEFORE HE NEEDS (Book #5)
BEFORE HE FEELS (Book #6)
BEFORE HE SINS (Book #7)
BEFORE HE HUNTS (Book #8)
BEFORE HE PREYS (Book #9)
BEFORE HE LONGS (Book #10)
BEFORE HE LAPSES (Book #11)
BEFORE HE ENVIES (Book #12)
BEFORE HE STALKS (Book #13)
BEFORE HE HARMS (Book #14)

**AVERY BLACK MYSTERY SERIES**

CAUSE TO KILL (Book #1)
CAUSE TO RUN (Book #2)
CAUSE TO HIDE (Book #3)
CAUSE TO FEAR (Book #4)
CAUSE TO SAVE (Book #5)
CAUSE TO DREAD (Book #6)

**KERI LOCKE MYSTERY SERIES**

A TRACE OF DEATH (Book #1)
A TRACE OF MURDER (Book #2)
A TRACE OF VICE (Book #3)
A TRACE OF CRIME (Book #4)
A TRACE OF HOPE (Book #5)

Manufactured by Amazon.ca
Acheson, AB

12990850R00099